CHILDREN'S CLASSICS

Oliver Twist

By
Charles Dickens

Adapted by
Mary Kerr

Edited by
Sophie Evans

Published by BK Books Ltd
First published in 2007
Copyright © BK Books Ltd

ISBN: 978-1-906068-44-8
Printed in China

Contents

Chapter 1

The Miserable Orphan

I n a public workhouse, a young woman gave birth to a fragile baby, who laid gasping and fighting for his life. An old nurse stood by, attending the infant. The doctor, who delivered him, feared that the child would not survive. Then all of a sudden, as if to contradict the doctor, the child gave out a feeble cry.

The baby's pale mother stretched out her hands and spoke in a faint voice, "Let me see the child."

The doctor placed the baby boy in the young woman's arms and she kissed the baby passionately upon its forehead, then fell back and passed away.

"It's all over, nurse!" said the doctor, after a while. "She was a good-looking girl; where did she come from?"

"She was brought here last night," replied the old woman, "by the overseer's order. She was found lying in the street; but where she came from, or where she was heading, nobody knows."

"I am guessing she was not married. There is no wedding ring on her finger," said the doctor.

Saying so, the doctor left the room to have his dinner, leaving the baby in the care of the workhouse people. The baby boy was named Oliver Twist.

But the workhouse could not find anyone who could take care of the child, so they sent infant Oliver to another workhouse. Oliver was only eight or nine months old when he was sent away.

Oliver spent the first nine years of his life in this workhouse with some twenty or thirty other impoverished children. An elderly woman called Mrs. Mann supervised this workhouse. She used to receive seven pence and half a penny per head, every week for the maintenance of the children. But the smart Mrs. Mann used to seize the greater part of the weekly payment for her own self. As a result, the children were malnourished; and the rags they wore were seldom washed.

So, it was not surprising that Oliver Twist's ninth birthday found him a pale and thin boy of a small stature. Lack of nourishment had not provided the child's body much opportunity for growth.

On this particular day, Oliver, along with two other boys, had been soundly beaten and locked up in the coal cellar. They were punished because they had dared to speak about their hunger. After this task was satisfactorily complete, Mrs. Mann was startled by the sudden appearance of Mr. Bumble, beadle of the parish. He was trying to unfasten the garden gate to enter inside.

Mr. Bumble's visit was completely unexpected, and Mrs. Mann hurried to welcome him. But before she went outside, she directed her maid to take Oliver and the other two boys out of the cellar and give them a bath.

"Goodness gracious! Is that you, Mr. Bumble?" Mrs. Mann cried out, pretending to be pleased. "What a pleasant surprise!"

Mr. Bumble was a middle-aged, fat and ill-tempered man. He did not care to respond to the greeting but gave the gate a tremendous kick. "Do you think this is respectful or proper conduct, Mrs. Mann," inquired Mr. Bumble, grasping his cane, "to keep the parish officers waiting at your garden gate?"

"Oh, I was only talking with a couple of dear children...oh! They are so fond of you, what a good and kind man you are!" replied Mrs. Mann, humbly.

"Well, well, it may be as you say," answered Mr. Bumble, immediately pacified. "I have come here, Mrs. Mann, to talk about a certain orphan you have here. Is it not that the child named Oliver Twist has turned nine today?"

"Bless him!" interposed Mrs. Mann.

"We have never been able to discover who his father is, or his mother's name," said Mr. Bumble.

"Oh really!" cried Mrs. Mann. "How did he get his name then?"

"I named him," Mr. Beadle answered, proudly. "We name our orphans in alphabetical order. The last was an '*S*', so I named him Swubble. Next was a '*T*', so I named him Twist. The next one will be Unwin and the next Vilkins. I have got all names ready up to *Z*."

"You are so knowledgeable, Mr. Bumble," cried Mrs. Mann.

"Well, well, I might be as you say," said the beadle, evidently pleased with the compliment. Then he further added, "As Oliver is now too old to remain here, the board has decided to send him back to the house where he was born. Today, I have come to take him back with me."

"I'll fetch him immediately," said Mrs. Mann, leaving the room.

By this time, Oliver had been properly washed and nicely dressed. Then, Mrs. Mann brought him before Mr. Bumble.

"Make a bow to the gentleman, Oliver," said Mrs. Mann.

"Will you go along with me, Oliver?" said Mr. Bumble, in a majestic voice.

Oliver was about to say 'yes,' when, glancing upward, he saw Mrs. Mann standing behind the beadle's chair, shaking her fist at him. Oliver understood what that meant. So, with a sad look on his face, the boy asked, "Will Mrs. Mann go with me?"

"No, she can't," replied Mr. Bumble. "But she is welcome to visit you sometimes."

The moment he said this, Oliver started crying. It was an easy task for Oliver to bring tears to his eyes, it was the result of years of hunger and ill-treatment.

Mrs. Mann embraced him again and again and then gave Oliver what he wanted a thousand times more, a piece of bread and butter. So, with the piece of bread in his hand and a cap on his head, Oliver went with Mr. Bumble to start a new life.

Reaching the workhouse, Mr. Bumble led Oliver into a large whitewashed room, where eight or ten fat gentlemen were sitting round a table. A particularly fat gentleman with a round and red face sat at the head of the table, in a high armchair.

"Bow to the board," said Mr. Bumble.

Oliver brushed away two or three tears that were lingering in his eyes and bowed to the board.

"What is your name, boy?" asked the gentleman in the high chair.

"Oliver, sir. Oliver Twist!"

"Oliver, do you know that you are an orphan?"

"What's that, sir?" inquired poor Oliver.

"The boy is a fool, I thought he was," said the gentleman in the white waistcoat.

"Hush!" said the gentleman who had spoken first. "You know you've got no father or mother and that you were brought up by the parish, don't you?"

"Yes, sir," replied Oliver.

"Well! You have come here to be educated and to learn a useful trade," he said.

"So you'll begin to pick oakum tomorrow morning, at six o' clock," added the surly gentleman in the white waistcoat.

"Yes...yes sir!" stammered Oliver.

Oliver then made a low bow to the board, as told by the beadle, and was taken away to a large ward. That night, Oliver lay down on his new rough, hard bed and sobbed himself to sleep.

Poor Oliver! Little did he know, as he lay asleep, that the board had reached a very important decision that very day! They had decided to cut the rations for the workhouse inmates to the barest minimum. As a result, a new diet chart was made for the inmates. From now on, the inmates were to be provided with only a thin gruel, three times a day. The only change was half a roll on Sundays and an onion twice a week.

In this way, the wise board members provided the poor an opportunity to starve slowly. At first, the measures proved a bit expensive for the workhouse as the large number of deaths, due to semi-starvation, increased the undertaker's bill. However, the number of workhouse inmates became gradually less and the board members were delighted.

The children had their meal in a large stone hall of the workhouse. The master, with the help of one or two women, served the meals. The children were served the watery gruel only once, except during festive times when they were given a loaf of bread too.

The bowls never needed washing. The hungry boys polished them with their spoons till they shone again. Oliver Twist and his companions continued to slowly starve for a few months. At last they got so fed up that the boys decided that one of them should walk up to the master, Mr. Limbkins, and ask for more food.

Oliver was chosen among the boys to talk to the master.

The evening arrived and the children took their places. After the master had served the gruel, the boys winked at Oliver. He slowly rose from his seat and, advancing to the master, bowl and spoon in hand, said, "Please, sir, I want some more."

The master was stunned! He looked in astonishment at the little rebel for some seconds, and then clung to the container holding the gruel for support. His assistants were shocked, and the boys, terrified.

"What!" the master managed to say at last.

"Please, sir," repeated Oliver, "can I have some more?"

The master threw the serving spoon at Oliver's head and screamed loudly for the beadle.

The matter was turned to the immediate attention of the board.

"That boy will be hanged," declared Mr. Limbkins. "I know that boy will be hanged."

And after a long discussion, the board members finally decided to put a notice outside the workhouse gate, offering a reward of five pounds to anyone who would take Oliver away and teach him a trade.

Chapter 2

'To Let'

For a whole week Oliver remained a grave prisoner in a dark and solitary room, consigned to him by the board. This was his punishment for the grave offence he had committed by asking for more gruel. He cried bitterly all day and at night he tried to sleep, crouching in the corner.

Then one morning, Mr. Gamfield, the chimney sweeper, happened to see the bill regarding Oliver, as he passed outside the gate. He read the bill carefully and then walked up to the man who was waiting at the gates in a white waistcoat.

"I can teach the boy how to be a good chimney sweeper," said Mr. Gamfield. "I was in search of an apprentice and I am ready to take him."

"Walk in," said the gentleman in the white waistcoat.

Mr. Gamfield followed the gentleman to the board.

The board then discussed the matter among themselves for a few minutes.

"We have considered your proposal and we don't approve of it as we don't think it's a very safe job," Mr. Limbkins finally told Mr. Gamfield.

But Mr. Gamfield bargained further and finally made the deal for three pounds and ten shillings. Mr. Bumble was at once instructed to bring Oliver Twist before the magistrate for signature and approval that very afternoon.

Little Oliver, to his amazement, was taken out from the dark solitary room and ordered to put on a clean shirt. He had hardly done this when Mr. Bumble brought him a bowl of gruel along with some bread.

When Oliver saw this, he began to cry.

'The board must have decided to kill me. That is why they are trying to fatten me up,' he thought.

"Don't make your eyes red, Oliver, but eat your food and be thankful," said Mr.

Bumble, pompously. "Here is a gentleman who wants to take you as an apprentice."

"An apprentice, sir!" cried Oliver, trembling.

"Yes, yes," said Mr. Bumble.

Tears rolled down the poor child's face, when he heard this and he sobbed bitterly.

"Come," said Mr. Bumble, "Wipe your eyes with the cuffs of your jacket."

On their way to the magistrate, Mr. Bumble instructed Oliver to look very happy. He also told him to say that he was not forced to go there.

When they arrived at the office, Mr. Bumble said aloud, "Now, Oliver, my dear, come to the gentleman."

It was a large room, with a great window. Behind a desk sat two old gentlemen. Mr. Limbkins and Mr. Gamfield both stood in front of the table on either side.

"This is the boy, my lord," said Mr. Bumble.

"Well," said the old gentleman, "I suppose he's fond of chimney-sweeping?"

"He loves it, Your Honor," replied Bumble. As he said this, he gave Oliver a pinch, to intimate that he had better not say that he didn't.

"And you, sir, will you treat him well and feed him?" asked the old man, looking towards Mr. Gamfield.

"When I said I will, I meant it," replied Mr. Gamfield, doggedly.

The old gentleman, fixing his spectacles more firmly on his nose, looked about him for the inkstand. It was the critical moment of Oliver's fate. Then, the magistrate suddenly happened to take notice of Oliver's pale and terrified face.

He laid down his pen and said, "My boy! You look pale and alarmed. What is the matter?"

"Stand a little away from him, beadle," said the other magistrate, laying aside the paper and leaning forward with an expression of interest. "Now, boy, what's the matter? Go on, tell us. Don't be afraid."

Oliver fell on his knees and, clasping his hands together, cried, "Send me back to the dark room, but please do not send me with this dreadful man."

And saying so, the poor child began to cry bitterly.

The old gentleman was shocked and moved by the condition of the little boy. He kept the papers aside and told Mr. Gamfield that he would not be allowed to take Oliver with him.

"Take the boy back to the workhouse and treat him kindly," he ordered Mr. Bumble.

The next morning, the public were once again informed that Oliver Twist was 'To Let', and that five pounds would be paid to anybody who would take possession of him.

Chapter 3

An Undertaker in the Making

Oliver had to spend a few more days at the workhouse. Several people came by to ask for him and finally it was Mr. Sowerberry, the undertaker of the parish, who was allowed, by the board, to have Oliver.

Mr. Sowerberry was a tall, thin man, dressed in a shabby black suit. When Mr. Bumble brought Oliver to him, the coffin-maker had just opened his shop and was making some entries in a book by the light of a candle.

"Oh! So, he is the boy," said Mr. Sowerberry, as he raised the candle above his head to get a better view of Oliver. "Mrs. Sowerberry, please come here a moment, my dear."

His wife emerged from a little room behind the shop.

"My dear," said Mr. Sowerberry, "this is the boy from the workhouse that I told you about."

Oliver bowed before Mrs. Sowerberry.

"Dear me!" said the undertaker's wife, "he's very small!"

"There, little bag of bones," she added, addressing Oliver, "go downstairs."

And then she pushed Oliver down a steep flight of stairs into a damp and dark stone cell that she called the 'kitchen'. Here, Oliver found an untidy girl who wore torn stockings and worn out shoes.

"Here, Charlotte," said Mr. Sowerberry, who had followed Oliver down, "Give this boy some of the cold meat that was put out for the dog."

Mrs. Sowerberry looked in horror as the famished boy hungrily ate the food put before him. When Oliver had finished eating, Mrs. Sowerberry led him upstairs with the words, "Your bed is under the counter amidst the coffins. Come along, don't keep me waiting."

Oliver followed his new mistress to the said room. After he had been left alone, Oliver set the lamp down and gazed timidly about him with a mixed feeling of awe and dread. This room was worse than the dark room in the workhouse. It was hot and gloomy with coffins of every size scattered around. And the place where Oliver's flock mattress was thrust, looked like a grave.

Oliver felt lonely and miserable. He had no family, no friends and no one to care for him. With these depressing thoughts, Oliver crept into his narrow bed and soon fell asleep.

He was awakened in the morning, by a loud kicking at the outside of the shop-door.

"Open the door!" cried the boy who was kicking it.

Oliver opened the door to find a big charity-boy sitting outside the doorway, eating a slice of bread and butter.

"I beg your pardon, sir," said Oliver, "did you knock?"

"I kicked," replied the charity-boy.

"Do you want a coffin, sir?" inquired Oliver, innocently.

At this, the charity-boy looked fiercely at him and said that Oliver would get a beating, if he cut jokes with his superiors in that way.

"I'm Mister Noah Claypole and you're going to work under me," said the charity-boy. "Take down the shutters, you idle young ruffian!"

Mr. Sowerberry came down soon after and took Oliver with him to show him how they worked.

Before long, Mr. Sowerberry took a liking to Oliver and decided to train him as a mute for children's funerals.

One day, he took the boy with him to attend a pauper's funeral. This was the first time that Oliver had attended any funeral.

He disliked the undertaker's job as he found it very sordid, but was too helpless to get himself out of it.

Oliver had to attend numerous funerals with Mr. Sowerberry before getting formally apprenticed to the trade. As expected by his master, Oliver gradually became an expert in his work. But success at work brought many enemies for Oliver.

Noah Claypole hated Oliver and so did Charlotte. The only friend Oliver had in the

Sowerberry household was Mr. Sowerberry. But Mrs. Sowerberry disliked this and therefore was deliberately mean to the boy.

One day, Noah went to the extent of insulting Oliver in the name of his mother and in spite of the warnings given by Oliver, continued to provoke him. At last, Oliver lost his temper. Crimson with fury, he overthrew the chair and table and seized Noah by the throat. Oliver shook Noah, till his teeth chattered in his head.

"He'll murder me!" screamed Noah. "Charlotte! Missis! Help! Oliver's gone mad!"

Mrs. Sowerberry and Charlotte came rushing to him.

"Oh, you little wretch!" screamed Charlotte and gave Oliver a blow with all her might.

In the meantime, Noah rose from the ground and struck Oliver from behind. All three of them hit the boy and locked him in the cellar.

"Run to Mr. Bumble, Noah," said Mrs. Sowerberry, "and tell him to come here immediately."

Noah Claypole ran along the streets as fast as he could, until he reached the workhouse.

"Oh, Mr. Bumble, sir!" cried Noah, "Oliver, sir, Oliver has..."

"What? What?" interposed Mr. Bumble. "Not run away, has he, Noah?"

"No, sir," replied Noah. "He tried to murder me, sir; and then he tried to murder Charlotte; and then the mistress!"

Mr. Bumble was horrified to hear Noah's version of the incident and was busy expressing his lamentations, when Mr. Limbkins happened to pass by. He heard Mr. Bumble lament and immediately asked him the reason for this.

"It's a boy from the free-school, sir," replied Mr. Bumble, "who has been nearly murdered by young Twist."

"I knew it!" cried Mr. Limbkins. "I knew from the very beginning that the young savage would be hanged some day!"

When Mr. Bumble reached the workhouse, he found that Oliver's clothes had been torn in the beating he had received, his face was bruised and scratched and his hair, scattered over his forehead.

The entire incident was narrated to Mr. Sowerberry when he arrived. Oliver glared boldly at Noah and looked quite undismayed.

"Now, you are a nice young fellow, aren't you?" said Mr. Sowerberry, giving Oliver a box on the ear.

"He called my mother names," replied Oliver.

"Well, and what if he did, you little ungrateful wretch?" said Mrs. Sowerberry. "She deserved what he said."

"She didn't!" cried Oliver.

"She did," said Mrs. Sowerberry.

"It's a lie!" cried Oliver.

Mrs. Sowerberry now burst into a flood of tears.

This flood of tears was nothing more then a ploy employed to make sure that Oliver got a beating from Mr. Sowerberry. The undertaker had no other alternative but to thrash the poor boy. Mr. Bumble too, followed suit and gave Oliver a generous beating with his cane.

For the remaining day, Oliver was shut up in the back kitchen with just a piece of stale bread. At night, he was ordered into his dismal bed, where he sat absolutely motionless for a long time. Only silent tears rolled down his grimy cheeks.

Later, before the break of dawn, Oliver suddenly arose, opened the door and, with one hesitant look around, ran out of the house.

Chapter 4

London – Oliver's Hideout

O liver ran and at times hid behind the hedges, fearing that he might be pursued and overtaken. Then, at noon, he sat down to rest by the side of a milestone and began to think as to where he should go. Suddenly, his eyes fell on the milestone that said, 'Seventy Miles to London.'

Oliver thought, 'London! Nobody, not even Mr. Bumble, could ever find me in London!' Oliver had heard, at the workhouse, that London was a vast city and there were various ways a person could hide there. Therefore, he decided to go to London and make a living there on his own.

Oliver walked for seven days, when finally, he reached a small town on the outskirts of London. Tired and hungry, he sat down by the roadside. As he sat looking at the taverns around him and the carriages passing by, a young man walked up to him and looked at him enquiringly.

"Hello friend! Why are you sitting here all alone?"

He was a dirty, snub-nosed, flat-browed, common-faced boy. But he had about him the arrogance and manners of a man. With little, sharp, ugly eyes and bowlegs, the boy was short for his age. He wore a hat and a coat that reached down to his heels.

"I am hungry and tired and have walked for the past seven days," said Oliver.

As he said this, tears rolled down the child's eyes and he began sobbing.

"Seven days!" exclaimed the boy. "Well, come along, you must be hungry, we'll get you something to eat."

The young gentleman took Oliver to a nearby shop and bought him some ham and bread. Then he took Oliver to a tavern and ordered some beer for himself. Oliver had a hearty meal for the first time in his life.

"Going to London?" said the strange boy, when Oliver had at last finished his meal.

"Yes."

"Got any lodgings?"

"No."

"Money?"

"No."

"Don't worry," said the young gentleman. "I'm going to London tonight and I know a respectable old gentleman who lives there. He'll let you stay in his house for free if I introduce you to him."

As night fell, they walked towards the great city. On the way, Oliver got to know that the name of his new friend was Jack Dawkins, better known as 'The Artful Dodger'.

They passed a narrow, muddy lane, which was full of drunken men. The air in the lane smelled foul. Suddenly, Jack stopped in front of a door, pushed it open and pulled Oliver inside by his arm. Then he groped his way up a dark and broken staircase, closely followed by Oliver and threw open the door of a back room. The walls and ceiling of the room were absolutely black with age and dirt. There was a table before the fireplace and upon the table was a candle stuck in a ginger-beer bottle, a loaf, butter and a plate. Some sausages were cooking in a frying pan. A shriveled old man dressed in a dirty flannel gown stood near them with a toasting fork in his hand. He had thick, matted, red hair and a very ugly face. Huddled side by side on the floor, were several rough beds made of old sacks. The only other furniture in the room was a clotheshorse, where a few handkerchiefs were hung. In one corner of the room were four or five boys, none older than the Dodger, smoking long clay pipes. All the boys huddled around Jack, as he whispered something to them and to the old man. Then he turned and smiled at Oliver.

"Fagin, this is my friend Oliver Twist," Jack Dawkins announced.

Fagin, too, grinned and shook hands with Oliver. The young boys came round him and shook both his hands very hard.

"We are very glad to see you, Oliver," said Fagin. "Dodger, take off the sausages and draw a tub near the fire for Oliver."

All the boys sat down for supper. Oliver ate his share with a glass of gin and water. Immediately after drinking it, Oliver felt himself gently lifted on to one of the sacks and then he fell into a deep sleep.

It was late next morning when Oliver awoke from a long and sound sleep. The room was empty but for Fagin, who was boiling some coffee in a saucepan for breakfast and whistling to himself.

Although Oliver had roused himself from sleep, he was not thoroughly awake. He saw the man through his half-closed eyes.

When the coffee was done, Fagin drew the saucepan to the hob and then turned round to look at Oliver. When he was convinced that Oliver was asleep, the old man stepped gently to the door and then drew out a small box from some trap in the floor. He placed the box on the table, raised the lid and looked in. Then he took out from it watches, rings, brooches, bracelets and other articles of jewelry, made of such magnificent materials.

Suddenly, Fagin's eyes fell on Oliver's face and he saw that the boy's eyes were fixed on him in silent curiosity. He closed the lid of the box with a loud crash and jumped up.

"What's that?" said the man. "Why do you watch me like that? What have you seen? Speak out, boy! Quick - quick! Don't keep me waiting!"

"I wasn't able to sleep any longer, sir," replied Oliver, meekly. "I am very sorry if I have disturbed you, sir."

"Of course I know that, my dear," said Fagin, immediately altering his tone. "I only tried to frighten you. Ha! Ha! You're a brave boy, Oliver."

The old man rubbed his hands and laughed to himself, all the while glancing uneasily at the box. "Did you see those pretty things, my dear?" he said, laying his hand upon the box.

"Yes, sir," replied Oliver.

"Ah!" said the man, turning rather pale. "Oliver, they are all I have to live upon. I am saving them for my old age."

Oliver thought that Fagin was a miser because he lived in such a dirty place in spite of all the riches he had saved, but then he thought that perhaps Fagin's fondness for the Dodger and the other boys cost him a good deal of money. So Oliver only cast him a respectful look and asked if he might get up.

"Certainly, my dear, certainly," replied Fagin. "First, wash yourself up and then have your breakfast."

Oliver had scarcely washed himself, when the Dodger returned, accompanied by a young man whom the Dodger introduced as Charley Bates.

"What have you got, Dodger?" asked the old man.

"A couple of pocket-books," replied Dodger.

"And what have you got, my dear?" said Fagin to Charley Bates.

"Four pocket-handkerchiefs," replied master Bates.

"Well," said Fagin, inspecting the handkerchiefs closely, "they're very good ones. You have marked them well though, Charley; so the marks shall be picked out with a needle and we'll teach Oliver how to do it."

"Oliver, you'd like to be able to make pocket-handkerchiefs as easily as Charley Bates, wouldn't you, my dear?"

"If you'll teach me, sir," replied Oliver.

At this reply, everyone started laughing loudly, but Oliver could not understand why.

Then the four had a nice breakfast of coffee, hot rolls and ham.

After the breakfast had been cleared away, Fagin and the two boys played a very curious game. The old man put a snuffbox, a wallet, a watch and other valuable things in his waistcoat pocket. Then he walked briskly up and down the room with a stick, imitating the old gentlemen on the streets. Sometimes he stopped, pretending to stare into shop-windows. All this while, the two boys followed him closely about and at last, the Dodger trod upon his toes, while Charley Bates stumbled up behind him and in that one moment they took from him, with the most extraordinary rapidity, the snuff-box, note-case and all the other valuables. If Fagin felt a hand in his pocket he would cry out and then the game would start all over again.

When this game had been played a great many times, a couple of young ladies came in, one of whom was named Bet and the other, Nancy. They were remarkably free and agreeable in their manners and Oliver thought them to be very nice girls.

After a while of talking, Nancy and Bet left, along with Dodger and Charley Bates.

"Now, my dear," said Fagin, "Is my handkerchief hanging out of my pocket?"

"Yes, sir," said Oliver.

"See if you can take it out, without my feeling it, as you saw the boys do earlier this morning."

So, Oliver held up the bottom of Fagin's pocket with one hand, as he had seen the Dodger hold it and drew the handkerchief lightly out of it with the other hand.

"Do you have it?" cried Fagin.

"Here it is, sir," said Oliver, showing the handkerchief in his hand.

"You're a clever boy, my dear," said Fagin, patting Oliver on the head approvingly. "I never saw a more intelligent boy. Here's a shilling for you."

Chapter 5

Oliver Becomes Aware
of Fagin's Business

O liver practiced this trick for many days and finally was allowed by Fagin to go out with the Dodger and Charley Bates.

On Oliver's first day at work, the three boys were standing on the roadside when, all at once, Oliver's companions began following an old gentleman, who had come out of a bookstall. Dodger and Bates asked Oliver to wait, watch and learn.

As Oliver looked on, he was horrified to see the Dodger put his hand into the old gentleman's pocket and draw from there a handkerchief! Then both of them ran away.

Suddenly, Oliver realized what kind of 'work' Fagin and his boys actually did! He grew terrified and started running as fast as he could.

Now, in the very instant when Oliver began to run, the old gentleman put his

hand to his pocket and found it empty. He immediately turned around sharply. When he saw Oliver running, he shouted, "Stop that thief!"

Everybody on the road started chasing the boy.

At last, the exhausted boy fell down on the pavement, hit by a tremendous blow. He was covered with mud and dust and bleeding from the mouth. At this point, a police officer made his way through the crowd and pulled Oliver to his feet. He was thoroughly searched, but nothing was found on his person. Then the officer took Oliver to a stone cell and locked him inside.

Meanwhile, Mr. Brownlow, the old gentleman whose handkerchief had been stolen, had been thinking, 'There is something familiar in that boy's face, something that touches and interests me. Can he really be innocent?'

Shortly after, Oliver Twist was presented before Mr. Fang, the magistrate.

Mr. Brownlow, who was present in the court, requested the magistrate that since he had only seen the boy running and not actually stealing, he should be dealt with leniently. Moreover, the boy looked rather pale and ill.

And then, as he stood there in front of the magistrate, Oliver fainted with sickness and fright.

"Take care of him, officer," said Mr. Brownlow, raising his hands instinctively.

However, the men in the office merely looked at each other without moving. The despair of the sick and injured child failed to move the hardhearted men.

Mr. Fang sentenced Oliver to three months hard labor. But just as the officers were preparing to carry the unconscious Oliver to his cell, an elderly man rushed hastily into the office, and cried out, "Stop, stop! Don't take him away!"

"What is this? Turn this man out. Clear the office!" cried Mr. Fang.

"Let me speak," cried the man; "I saw it all happen. I am the owner of the bookstall. I saw three boys; two others and the prisoner here were hanging around on the opposite side of the way. The companions of this little boy committed the robbery and I saw that your prisoner here was perfectly amazed and shocked by it," said the man.

"Why didn't you come here before?" asked Mr. Fang.

"There was nobody to take care of my shop. The moment I was able to free myself, I rushed here."

After this testimony, Oliver Twist was cleared of all the charges.

As Mr. Brownlow walked out of the magistrate's chamber, he saw little Oliver lying on his back on the pavement, his forehead filled with perspiration and his face a ghostly white.

"Poor boy, poor boy!" said Mr. Brownlow, bending over him. "Somebody please call a coach."

A coach was got and Oliver was carefully laid on the seat. Mr. Brownlow, too, got in and they drove away.

Chapter 6

Life with the Brownlows

The coach stopped before Mr. Brownlow's house. Mr. Brownlow carried Oliver inside and carefully lay him down on the bed that had been quickly prepared for him.

Oliver suffered from high fever and remained unconscious for many days. After several days, weak and pale, he regained consciousness and saw a motherly old lady standing by his bed. All of a sudden, out of fear and anxiety Oliver started crying.

"Hush, my dear," said the old lady softly. "You must be quiet, or you will be ill again. Lie down, lie down."

With these words, the old lady very gently placed Oliver's head upon the pillow and looked so very kindly at him that it brought tears to the eyes of the little boy who had faced neglect and unkindness all his life. The old lady brought some cool stuff for Oliver to drink. And soon, the boy fell into a gentle doze.

The next day, when Oliver woke up, he felt cheerful and happy. In three days' time, he was able to sit in an easy chair, with many pillows. As he was still too weak to walk, the old woman, who was called Mrs. Bedwin, had him carried downstairs into the little housekeeper's room, which belonged to her.

"You're very, very kind to me, ma'am," said Oliver.

"Well, never mind that, my dear," said Mrs. Bedwin; "Mr. Brownlow may come in to see you this morning and we must look our best, because the better we look, the more pleased he'll be."

During all this time, Oliver looked at the portrait of a beautiful lady that hung on the wall.

"Are you fond of pictures, dear?" inquired Mrs. Bedwin, seeing that Oliver had fixed his eyes attentively on the portrait.

"I do not know about that madam, but that lady has a beautiful face!" said Oliver, without taking his eyes from the canvas.

"Yes," said Mrs. Bedwin, "that's a portrait."

"Whose, ma'am?" asked Oliver.

"Well, my dear, I do not know," answered Mrs. Bedwin in good humor. But these words were not enough to satisfy Oliver's curiosity. The picture still remained in his mind.

Meanwhile, Mrs. Bedwin broke bits of toasted bread into some soup and handed it to Oliver. The boy had scarcely swallowed the last spoonful when they heard a soft tap on the door.

"Come in," said Mrs. Bedwin and in walked Mr. Brownlow.

Now, when the old gentleman came in, Oliver, out of respect, made an attempt to stand up, but sloped back in his seat the next moment, as he was very weak.

"Poor boy!" said Mr. Brownlow, clearing his throat. "How do you feel, my dear?"

"Very happy, sir," replied Oliver, "and very grateful indeed, sir, for your goodness to me. I hope you are not angry with me, sir?" Oliver said further, raising his eyes earnestly.

"Oh, no," replied Mr. Brownlow, hastily shifting his eyes from the child's innocent stare.

"Why! What's this? Mrs. Bedwin, look there!" As Mr. Brownlow spoke, he pointed hastily to the picture over Oliver's head and then to the boy's face. There was a striking *similarity*! The eyes, the head, the mouth; every feature was the same!

A few days later, when Oliver was talking to Mrs. Bedwin, there came a message from Mr. Brownlow asking Oliver to meet him in the study. Accordingly, Oliver went down to the study dressed in his new suit, new cap and new pair of shoes, that Mr. Brownlow had custom made for him. Oliver found Mr. Brownlow sitting with another gentleman in the study. This old gentlemen was a friend of Mr. Brownlow and his name was Mr. Grimwig.

"This is young Oliver Twist, whom we were speaking about," said Mr. Brownlow.

Oliver bowed.

"How are you, boy?" said Mr. Grimwig, looking intently at Oliver.

"A great deal better, thank you, sir," replied Oliver.

At that moment, Mrs. Bedwin happened to bring in a small parcel of books, which Mr. Brownlow had purchased that morning. Having laid them on the table, she prepared to leave the room.

"Stop the book-store boy, Mrs. Bedwin!" said Mr. Brownlow. "There are a few books that I need to send back."

"He has left, sir," replied Mrs. Bedwin.

"Send Oliver with them," put in Mr. Grimwig, with an ironical smile and a meaningful glance at Mr. Brownlow. "He will be able to deliver them safely, you know."

"Yes, allow me take them, if you please, sir," said Oliver, eager to be of use. "I'll run all the way, sir."

"All right then Oliver, take the books and come back soon," said Mr. Brownlow.

"It won't take ten minutes, sir," said Oliver eagerly and ran out with the books under his arm.

"Oh! So you expect him to come back, do you?" inquired Mr. Grimwig.

"I do! Don't you?" asked Mr. Brownlow, smiling.

"No," Mr. Grimwig said, "I do not. You do not know who he is or where he came from! The boy has a new suit of clothes on his back and a set of valuable books under his arm. He'll join his old friends, the thieves, and laugh at you. I don't think that the boy is going to come back, sir."

With these words, he drew his chair closer to the table and there the two friends sat, in silent expectation. It grew very dark, but there the two old gentlemen sat patiently waiting. But there was no sign of Oliver.

On the other hand, Fagin got very angry when the Dodger and Charley Bates returned without Oliver.

"Where's Oliver?" said Fagin. "Where's the boy?"

"The officers got him," said the Dodger, grimly.

The moment the Dodger had said this, a loud noise came from downstairs and a deep voice growled, "What is all this about, Fagin?"

The man who had said these words was stoutly built, about thirty-five years old. He had a dirty handkerchief round his neck. He was called Bill Sikes, one of Fagin's gang members.

When Sikes heard about Oliver's capture, he was very angry with Fagin. He felt that Fagin had let Oliver go out without training him properly.

"I hope he does not say anything about us," said Fagin, anxiously.

"That's very likely," returned Sikes, with a wicked grin. "I suggest that someone should be sent to the police station to find out what happened to the little boy."

However, the next question was who would go to the police station to get information regarding Oliver. Fagin and the boys could not go because they would be arrested.

Finally, after some discussion, Nancy was persuaded to do the job. So, Nancy reached the police station as they had planned and went straight to an officer in a striped waistcoat and cried out, "Where is my brother? Where is my little brother?"

"I haven't got him, my dear," said the officer.

"Then where is he?" screamed Nancy, in a distracted manner.

"Why, the gentleman's got him," replied the officer.

"What gentleman? Oh, gracious heavens! What gentleman?" exclaimed Nancy.

"The gentleman from Pentonville."

Chapter 7

Oliver is Kidnapped

Meanwhile, by mistake Oliver had taken the wrong path. As he was walking along, he felt a pair of arms thrown tightly around his neck.

"Don't!" cried Oliver, struggling. "Let me go! Who is it?"

The woman who had grabbed him cried out loudly, "Oh my gracious! I have found him! Oh! Oliver! Oh you naughty boy, you make me suffer greatly! Come home. Oh, I've found him!"

Hearing her cries, a few women had gathered around them.

"Oh, ma'am," said the young woman to one in the crowd, "he ran away from his parents almost a month ago, and went and joined a gang of thieves and broke his mother's heart."

"You naughty child!" one of the women told Oliver. "Go home to your mother."

"I don't know her!" wailed Oliver. "I do not have any sister, or father or mother either. I'm an orphan and I live at Pentonville."

And then, suddenly, Oliver saw the woman's face.

"Why, it's Nancy!" exclaimed Oliver.

"You see, he knows me!" cried Nancy, appealing to the bystanders.

Suddenly, a man stepped out of a nearby shop and pulled Oliver in, along with Nancy.

It was Bill Sikes.

"I don't know them. Help! Help!" cried Oliver loudly, struggling in the man's powerful grasp.

Weak with recent illness, poor Oliver could not do anything to rescue himself from his kidnappers. Oliver knew that he was once again lost in the dark alleys of London.

The gas-lamps were still lighted. Mrs. Bedwin was standing at the open door, waiting anxiously for Oliver. The servant had run up the street twenty times to see if there were any traces of Oliver. Mr. Brownlow stayed awake waiting for him, but Oliver did not come back to him.

Bill Sikes, Nancy and Sikes' dog, Bull's Eye, led Oliver back to Fagin.

"Here he is!" cried out Charley Bates when he saw Oliver. "Oh, Fagin, look at him! Do look at him! Hold me, somebody, while I laugh it out. Elegant clothes and books in hand. Oliver is a gentleman, Fagin!"

"I am delighted to see you looking so well, my dear," said Fagin, bowing to Oliver with mock humility. "Why didn't you write, my dear, to tell us that you were coming? We'd have prepared something warm for supper."

The next moment Bates laughed so loud that even the Dodger could not help but smile.

A minute later, Fagin snatched all the books from Oliver's grasp.

"Please do not take the books, they belong to the kind, old gentleman," pleaded Oliver, wringing his hands. "The good, old gentleman took me into his house and had me nursed, when I was dying of fever. He'll think I stole the books. The old lady and all of the others who were so kind to me will think I stole them and have gone back to my friends! Oh, do have mercy upon me and send them back!"

With these words, Oliver fell upon his knees at Fagin's feet.

"You are right, Oliver," chuckled Fagin, "they will think you stole them and never look for you again! Ha! Ha!"

Suddenly, Oliver jumped to his feet and tore wildly from the room, uttering shrieks for help.

"Stop, or I will set the dog on you!" cried Sikes, angrily.

"Keep back the dog, Bill!" cried Nancy. "He'll tear the boy to pieces. You've got the boy and what more would you have? If you do anything to him, I will go to the police station and confess all my crimes."

The girl stamped her foot violently on the floor as she said this.

Fagin saw that Nancy would actually do as she threatened and so asked Sikes to keep the dog back and then sent Oliver to bed.

Chapter 8

Mr. Bumble Comes to London City

A few days after Nancy and Sikes had kidnapped Oliver, Mr. Bumble visited London for some work. As he was walking down the street he saw a notice:

'**FIVE GUINEAS REWARD**

A YOUNG BOY NAMED OLIVER IS MISSING FROM PENTONVILLE. ANYONE GIVING ANY INFORMATION REGARDING HIS LIFE OR LEADING TO HIS DISCOVERY WILL BE REWARDED WITH FIVE GUINEAS.'

FIVE GUINEAS
REWARD.

A YOUNG BOY NAMED
OLIVER TWIST IS MISSING
FROM PENTONVILLE. ANY
ONE GIVING ANY
INFORMATION REGA-
RDING HIS LIFE OR
LEADING TO HIS DISCO-
VERY WILL BE REW-
ARDED WITH FIVE
GUINEAS

Oliver's description and the address of Mr. Brownlow were given below it.

Mr. Bumble immediately went to Mr. Brownlow's house, and found him in the study, along with his friend, Mr. Grimwig.

When Mr. Bumble had introduced himself and explained the reason behind his visit, Mr. Brownlow inquired, "Do you know where this poor boy is now?"

"No sir," replied Mr. Bumble.

Then he told the two gentlemen that Oliver was born of low parents, that he had been a liar and an ungrateful fellow from a young age. He told them that Oliver had attacked another boy and then had run away in the middle of the night from his master's house. Mr. Bumble then showed the two gentlemen some legal papers that confirmed that he knew Oliver.

"I fear it is all too true," said old Mr. Brownlow sadly, when he had examined the papers. He gave Mr. Bumble the money as promised, adding regretfully, "I would gladly have given you more money, if your account had been more favorable to the boy."

Once Mr. Bumble had left, Mr. Brownlow rang the bell violently.

"Mrs. Bedwin," said Mr. Brownlow, when the housekeeper appeared; "that boy, Oliver, is a liar and a thief."

"Pardon me, sir but I would never believe it," replied the old lady. "He was a dear, grateful, gentle child."

"He is not!" cried Mr. Brownlow, trying to hide his anguish. "I rang to tell you that, Mrs. Bedwin. Never let me hear the boy's name again. Remember! Never!"

Chapter 9

The Foiled Robbery

O ne cold, damp night, shortly after Oliver's return, Fagin went to see Sikes at his house.

"Well?" said Sikes, as Fagin entered the room.

"I came to talk to you about the robbery at Chertsey," he spoke in a very low voice.

"Yes. What about it?" inquired Sikes.

"When are you going to do it?" asked Fagin. "It is going to bring us a lot of riches. I think you should plan it soon."

"Well, the problem is that nobody from the house is ready to help us. The servants are very loyal. I think we will have to manage with our own people if we are to do it," said Sikes.

"All right then, let's do it," said Fagin.

"But there is one more problem. I would need a small boy to get in through a small window," Sikes said.

"That is no problem! I have the right boy for you. Oliver is the right size for your work. And I believe he will do it if you frighten him well enough," said Fagin.

"Well, it is settled then," said Sikes. "But remember, you won't see him alive again, Fagin, if anything goes wrong because of him. Mark my words!"

"When is it to be done?" asked Nancy, who was listening quietly all through.

"Toby and I have planned it for the day after tomorrow, at night," said Sikes.

"Good," said Fagin, "it will be a moonless night."

The next evening, Nancy came to take Oliver to Sikes' place.

Oliver saw that the girl looked very pale and gently inquired if she were ill. But she merely sat down on a chair and made no reply. "Oh God, forgive me!" she cried after a while, "I never thought of this."

She rocked herself to and fro, caught her throat, and, uttering a gurgling sound, gasped for breath.

"Nancy!" cried Oliver, frightened, "What is it?"

Suddenly, Nancy stopped moaning, drew her shawl close round her and shivered with cold. She kept sitting for a while without uttering a single word. Then all of a sudden, she raised her head and looked at Oliver.

"I don't know what comes over me sometimes," said she. "Now, dear, are you ready?"

"Where are you taking me to?" asked Oliver.

"I am taking you to Bill Sikes," replied Nancy.

"What for?" asked Oliver, drawing back.

"For no good!" replied Nancy. "Oh, Oliver, I have promised that you would be quiet and silent; if you are not, they are going to harm you and me. They will perhaps even kill me. I would love to help you, but I have no power. So just follow what Bill tells you to!"

Hearing this, Oliver held Nancy's hand and silently walked with her to Sikes' house.

Next morning, at about five o'clock, Bill Sikes and Oliver left the house.

Oliver was given a handkerchief to tie round his throat and a large, rough cape to button over his shoulders. Before leaving the house, Sikes showed the terrified boy a pistol hidden in a side-pocket of his coat. This he did with a threatening gesture.

Oliver wondered repeatedly, as they kept walking, as to where his companion meant to take him. The two walked the entire day and it had grown quite dark when they reached the foot of a bridge.

A damp mist rose from the river. The marshy ground spread itself over the dreary fields and it was bitterly cold. All around was gloomy and black. As they reached near the bank, Oliver suddenly became fearful.

'The water!' he thought. 'He has brought me to this lonely place to murder me!'

Oliver was about to throw himself on the ground and make one last attempt to save his young life, when he saw that they stood before a solitary, old and decaying house. The house was dark and looked uninhabited.

Sikes held on to Oliver's hand, opened the door and went in. They passed through a gloomy passage and entered a low, dark room with a smoky fire, two or three broken chairs and a table. There was also a very old couch, on which a man was resting, smoking a long clay pipe. He was Toby Crackit.

"Bill Sikes!" cried Toby, "Come in, come in. Who's this?" he asked, as his eyes fell on Oliver.

"The boy!" replied Sikes, and then, stooping over Toby, he whispered something in his ear.

All this time, Oliver had been looking at Sikes in mute and timid wonder. He was frightened and terrified that he couldn't understand what was going on around him.

In a while, Toby brought some supper for them and then, after they had their supper, they all fell asleep. Oliver slept quite heavily until Toby Crackit, jumping up and declaring that it was half-past one, suddenly awakened him. Rapidly, Sikes and his companion covered their necks and chins in large dark shawls, put on their long coats and armed themselves with pistols. Then, all of them set out into the dark and foggy night.

After walking for a while, they finally stopped before a detached house surrounded by a wall. Toby immediately climbed the wall and called out for Oliver. Before Oliver could understand anything, Sikes had caught him under the arms and in three or four seconds he and Toby were lying on the grass on the other side of the wall. Sikes followed them and then they crept cautiously towards the house.

And now, for the first time, Oliver saw that *robbery* and maybe even *murder* was the object of the expedition! He clasped his hands together, a mist came before his eyes, his limbs failed him and he sank upon his knees and prayed. "Oh! For God's sake, let me go!" he cried. "Let me run away and die in the fields. I will never come near London! Oh! Please have mercy on me and do not make me become part of this robbery. Have mercy upon me!"

"Get up!" hissed Sikes, trembling with rage and aiming the pistol at Oliver's head. Toby placed his hand upon the boy's mouth and dragged him to the back of the house.

They now stood below a small window, about five and a half feet above the ground.

"Now listen," Sikes whispered to Oliver, drawing a dark lantern from his pocket, "I'm going to put you through there. Take this light; go softly up the steps and along the little hall to the street door. Then open it and let us in. And if you are not able to reach the bolt on the door, then stand on a chair and open it."

In a while, Oliver had crept through the window and landed safely on the floor inside. Sikes handed him a lantern through the window. However, in the meantime, Oliver had other thoughts. He had decided that he would try to wake the people of the house, even if he died in the process. As he was nervously climbing the stairs, suddenly Sikes cried out, "Come back! Come back!"

Scared by the sudden cry, Oliver let his lantern fall. He did not know whether to run away or go upstairs.

Sikes cried out again. At the same moment, two terrified, half-dressed men appeared at the top of the stairs –there was a sudden flash followed by a loud bang and then a crash was heard. Oliver staggered back.

Sikes' head had disappeared from the window for an instant; but he was up again and he pulled Oliver up by the collar before the smoke had cleared away. He fired his own pistol after the men who were already receding, and dragged the boy up.

"Clasp your arm tighter," said Sikes, as he drew Oliver through the window. "Give me a shawl here. They've hit the boy and he is bleeding!"

As Sikes took Oliver out, he could hear the loud bell ringing and the dogs barking, awakening the whole house and the neighborhood. Sikes picked up the unconscious boy in his arms and the two robbers ran for their lives.

Chapter 10

A Secret is Revealed

T he night was bitterly cold. The snow lay on the ground, frozen into a hard thick crust.

Such was the condition of the weather outside. Mrs. Corney, the matron of the workhouse in which Oliver Twist was born, and Mr. Bumble sat before a cheerful fire in Mrs. Corney's little room, drinking tea.

Suddenly, there was a hasty knock at the door.

The matron opened the door and very rudely asked the caller about her business.

"If you please, mistress," said a withered old female, putting her head in at the door, "Old Sally is going to die. She says she has got something to tell you. Can you please come fast?"

Mrs. Corney was quite annoyed at being disturbed during her conversation with Mr. Bumble. Nevertheless, she picked up a thick shawl and quickly rushed out with the old woman.

Old Sally was lying in an attic room. A dim light was burning at the farther end of the room. Two old women and an attendant were standing by Old Sally's bedside. The attendant nodded to Mrs. Corney to come over.

"If she lasts a couple of hours, I shall be surprised," said the attendant, as he walked out of the room.

At this moment, the patient raised herself upright, and stretched out her arms.

"Lie down, lie down!" cried Mrs. Corney crossly, going over to the woman's bedside.

"I'll never lie down again alive!" said the woman. "I will tell you! Come here! Nearer! Let me whisper in your ear."

She clutched the matron by the arm and was about to speak, when she looked round and caught sight of the two women

bending forwards, ready to eavesdrop on the conversation.

"Turn them away," said the woman, drowsily, "quick! Quick!"

The matron pushed them from the room, closed the door, and returned to the bedside.

"Now listen to me," said the dying woman, aloud. "In this very room, in this very bed, I once nursed a pretty young creature. She was brought into the house with her feet cut and bruised with walking. She gave birth to a boy and died."

"What about her?" asked Mrs. Corney, impatiently.

"Well," murmured the sick woman, "I robbed her, I did!"

"Stole what?" cried the matron.

"It!" replied the woman. "The only thing she had. She had kept it safe. Gold! Rich gold!"

"Gold!" echoed the matron, bending eagerly over the woman as she fell back. "Go on, go on. Who was the mother? Where is it?"

"She asked me to keep it safe," replied the woman with a groan. "Greed entered my heart from the moment I laid my eyes on it, hanging round her neck. They would have treated the child better, if they had known it all!"

"Known what?" asked the other. "Speak!"

"The boy grew so like his mother," said the woman, rambling on and not paying attention to the question, "that I could never forget it when I saw his face. Poor girl! She was so young, too! Wait, there's more to tell. I have not told you all, have I?"

"No, no," replied the matron. "Be quick, or it may be too late!"

"The mother," said the old woman, making a violent effort; "the mother said that a day might come when the child would not feel ashamed to hear its poor young mother's name."

"What was the boy's name?" demanded the matron.

"They called him Oliver," replied the woman, feebly. "The gold I stole was…"

"Yes, yes–what?" cried the matron.

She was bending eagerly over the ailing woman to hear her reply, but drew back, as the old woman muttered something and fell lifeless on the bed.

"Stone dead! And nothing to tell, after all," the matron declared carelessly to the two old women who had rushed inside the room. As she walked away, the matron took a small piece of paper out of the dead woman's hands.

Chapter 11

Fagin Plans with Monks

F agin was eagerly waiting to hear about the robbery, when Toby Crackit rushed into the room and dropped into a nearby chair.

"The robbery failed," Toby informed Fagin.

"I knew it," replied Fagin, angrily. "But there is more to tell, isn't there? Go on, what's the bad news?"

"They fired and hit the boy. We ran over the fields at the back, with him between us.

They pursued us. The whole country was awake and the dogs were set upon us."

"Where is he?" cried Fagin. "Where is Oliver?"

"Bill had him on his back and ran like the wind. We stopped to take him between us; his head hung down, and he was cold. They were close upon our heels. We parted company and left the youngster lying in a ditch. Whether he is alive or dead, we do not know."

Fagin uttered a loud cry and, twisting his hands in his hair, ran out of the room and out of the house.

Fagin rushed into an inn called the 'Three Cripples'. He looked eagerly at each face and finally, not finding the man he was looking for, went to the innkeeper and said in a whisper, "Is Monks here?"

"No," replied the man.

"Will he be here tonight?" asked Fagin.

"Certainly," replied the man. "If you'll wait ten minutes, he'll be here."

"No, no," said Fagin. "Tell him I came here to see him and that he must come and meet me tonight."

"Good!" said the man. "Nothing more?"

"Not a word now," said Fagin, as he descended the stairs of the inn.

As he reached the corner of the street, a dark figure emerged from the shadows.

"Fagin!" whispered a voice close to his ear.

"Ah!" said Fagin, turning quickly round, "Is that ..."

"Yes!" interrupted the stranger. "I have been lingering here for the last two hours. Where the devil have you been?"

"On your business, Monks," replied Fagin, "On your business all night."

Fagin and the stranger, whom Fagin had addressed as Monks, walked to Fagin's house. Fagin unlocked the door, and requested Monks to close it softly, while he lighted the lamp.

The two talked for some time in whispers. Then the stranger got angry and said loudly, "I tell you again, it was badly planned. Why did you not train the boy to become a pickpocket like the others?"

"I said it was not easy to train him in the business," replied Fagin. "He was not like the other boys."

"Remember, Fagin," said Monks, "I told you there should be no bloodshed. If the boy dies, I am not responsible in any way."

As Monks said this, he noticed a shadow on the opposite wall. Monks immediately nudged Fagin to keep quiet.

"Someone's there! Someone was listening to us!"

"What!" cried Fagin. "Where?"

"There!" Monks replied, glaring at the opposite wall. "The shadow! I saw the shadow of a woman wearing a cloak and a bonnet, pass by quickly."

They rushed out of the room, but didn't see anyone. They listened intently for any sound, but could hear nothing.

"Are you sure that you saw someone?" said Fagin, turning to his companion.

"Maybe; I am not sure," replied Monks.

As the clock struck one, the two parted.

Chapter 12

Mr. Bumble's Proposal
to Mrs. Corney

hen Mrs. Corney had gone to attend the dying patient, Mr. Bumble, left alone in the room, spent the entire time checking her possessions. When he checked her drawers, he found a small locked box. When he shook the box, Mr. Bumble heard the clinking of coins.

Smiling with satisfaction, Mr. Bumble returned with a stately walk to the fireplace.

"I'll do it!" he said, as if reaching some decision.

As Mr. Bumble was lost in his own thoughts, Mrs. Corney came hurrying back into the room. She threw herself on a chair by the fireside, gasping for breath. At the same time she covered her eyes with her hands.

"Please calm down my dear," said Mr. Bumble as he came rushing to her. "I will go

and fetch you a glass of wine. I am sure it will make you feel better," he said, and rushed to the cupboard to get her the drink.

"I feel better now," declared Mrs. Corney, after drinking half of it and falling back. "It's very comforting. Thank you so much for your kindness."

"You know that Mr. Slout is very ill and the doctor says he will not live for long," began Mr. Bumble, pompously. "He is the master of this establishment and his death will cause a vacancy. I could very well fill up that vacancy. Will you marry me then? We could live here together."

As Mr. Bumble said this, Mrs. Corney began sobbing.

"Please say 'Yes!'"

"Ye--ye--yes!" sighed the matron.

After matters had been agreeably and satisfactorily arranged, the two decided to celebrate with another glass of wine. While it was being disposed of, Mrs. Corney

acquainted Mr. Bumble with the old woman's demise.

"I'll call at Sowerberry's as I go home and tell him to send a coffin for Old Sally tomorrow morning," replied Mr. Bumble.

Mr. Bumble left the building with a light heart, which occupied his mind until he reached the shop of the undertaker. Then he made all necessary preparations for the old woman's funeral.

Chapter 13

The House of Maylie

"**M**ay the wolves tear your throats!" muttered Sikes, grinding his teeth and turning his head for an instant, to look back at his pursuers.

The loud shouting of men vibrated through the air in the mist and the darkness. The barking of the neighboring dogs, roused by the sound of the alarm bell, resounded in every direction.

"Stop! Give me a hand with the boy," cried Sikes, beckoning furiously to Toby

Crackit and trying to lay the injured boy in a dry ditch at his feet. The next moment, the noise grew louder. The men who were chasing the robbers were already climbing the gate of the field in which Sikes and Toby Crackit stood.

"It's all up, Bill!" cried Toby. "Drop the kid and run!"

Sikes clenched his teeth, took one look around, threw Oliver down and disappeared.

However, by then, the two men – Mr. Giles, the butler and steward to the

old lady of the house, and Brittles, an old servant – decided to return to the house.

As dawn approached, the air became cold and a light mist rolled on the ground like a cloud of dense smoke. Oliver lay motionless and insensible on the wet grass, where Sikes had left him. He still lay stretched, helpless and bleeding.

After a few hours, Oliver awoke, uttering a low cry of pain. He struggled to his feet and tried to walk. He saw that at no great distance there was a house and, gathering all his strength, staggered towards it.

As Oliver stood near the house, he realized that it was the same house they had attempted to rob last night. He pushed against the garden gate; it was unlocked. Oliver walked slowly across the lawn, climbed the steps, knocked faintly at the door and fell down unconscious, against one of the pillars of the porch.

Brittles heard the knock and opened the door. The moment he saw Oliver, he uttered a loud cry, making Mr. Giles rush towards him. Seeing the unconscious boy and recognizing him, Mr. Giles seized Oliver by one leg and one arm, dragged him straight into the hall and deposited him at full length on the floor.

"Here he is!" Giles called out in a state of great excitement. "Here's one of the thieves, Ma'am! Wounded, Miss! I shot him, Miss."

Two maids ran upstairs to tell the lady of the house that Mr. Giles had captured one of the robbers. Amid all the noise and commotion, a sweet female voice was heard.

"Giles!" called out the voice from the stair-head.

"I'm here, Miss," replied Mr. Giles.

"Is the poor creature much hurt?" enquired the young lady.

"Wounded badly, Miss," replied Giles.

"He looks as if he will not live," said Brittles. "Wouldn't you like to come and look at him, Miss?"

"Not now!" cried the young lady. "Oh! Treat him kindly, Giles, for my sake!"

The old servant looked up at the speaker, with an approving glance. Giles bent over Oliver and helped Brittles to carry him upstairs, with care and kindness.

Meanwhile, the lady of the house had instructed Brittles to go at once and fetch the family doctor. In half an hour, Brittles returned with a fat gentleman, who ran straight inside the house. He found two ladies eagerly awaiting his arrival. Of the two ladies, one was stately and middle aged. She was Mrs. Maylie, the lady of the house. The other was her niece, Rose Maylie, who was very beautiful and not more than seventeen years of age. The fat gentleman was Dr. Losberne, their family doctor.

The two women followed the doctor into the room where Oliver had been laid. The doctor stepped inside the room with the two ladies and closed the door behind him. Then he gently drew back the curtains of the bed. The two ladies had expected to see a rough-faced criminal upon the bed, but there lay a mere child, worn out with pain and exhaustion. His head reclined upon one arm, which was half hidden by his long hair, as it streamed over the pillow.

The three looked on, for a minute or so, in silence. Suddenly, the younger lady sat down on a chair by the bedside and gently pushed Oliver's hair from his face. As she stooped over him, her tears fell upon the unconscious boy's grubby forehead.

Oliver stirred and smiled in his sleep, as though these marks of sympathy and kindness had awakened some pleasant dream of a love and affection he had never known.

"How could this poor child have been the accomplice of robbers!" exclaimed Mrs. Maylie.

"How young he is!" cried Rose. "He may never have known a mother's love, or the comfort of a home. Ill-usage and hunger may have driven him to bad company. Please, dear aunt, do not send this sick child to prison, which might end all chances of his improvement."

"My dear child," said Mrs. Maylie, hugging the weeping girl, "do you think I would harm even a hair of his head? What can I do to save him, sir?" she asked the good doctor.

"I think we should first ask Giles and Brittles whether they were sure that they saw this boy with the robbers," answered Dr. Losberne.

However, when Dr. Losberne met the two servants and questioned Giles as to whether he was sure of the identity of Oliver as one of the robbers, the servant admitted that he was not very certain.

Accordingly, when the policemen came for the investigation of the attempted robbery, no one could identify the boy. So, Oliver was *off the hook*.

Chapter 14

Oliver's New Life

Oliver had a broken limb and his exposure to wet and cold had brought on a fever that persisted for many weeks. But, gradually, the boy regained his strength.

One day, Mrs. Maylie and Rose were sitting by his bedside. Oliver, in a few tearful words, thanked the two ladies for their kindness and for rescuing him from death and misery. Then, at the request of his two saviors, he recounted his entire sad history to them.

"Poor fellow!" said Rose, when Oliver struggled to utter his few words of thankfulness again. "You shall have many opportunities of serving us, if you will. We are going into the country and my aunt intends that you shall accompany us. In the quiet countryside, the pure air will help you become strong and healthy in a few days."

"Oh! Dear lady, if only I could work for you; if only I could repay you for all the kindness you have showered on me!" cried Oliver.

"We shall employ you in a hundred ways and I am sure you will make me very happy indeed," said Miss Maylie.

"Yes ma'am, I would be happy to do anything for you," cried Oliver.

When spring arrived, Oliver was taken to the Maylies' country cottage.

Oliver gradually began to get well and prospered under the united care of Mrs. Maylie, Rose and the kind-hearted Dr.

Losberne. The days Oliver spent there were the happiest in his life, since his stay with Mr. Brownlow.

Oliver had wanted for a long time to explain to Mr. Brownlow as to why he hadn't returned with his books. So, at Oliver's request, when he was healthy enough to make a journey, he and Dr. Losberne set out one morning towards Mr. Brownlow's house. Oliver remembered the street where

Mr. Brownlow resided. But, when they got there, they found the house empty and there was a notice on the window that said:

'*To Let.*'

Dr. Losberne knocked at the neighboring door and asked, "What has become of Mr. Brownlow, who used to live in the adjoining house?"

The servant of the house informed him that Mr. Brownlow had sold off his goods and gone to the West Indies, six weeks ago.

Oliver clasped his hands and sank feebly backward.

"Has his housekeeper gone too?" inquired Dr. Losberne, after a moment's pause.

"Yes, sir", replied the servant. "The old gentleman, the housekeeper and a gentleman who was a friend of Mr. Brownlow's, all went together."

"Then turn towards home again," said Dr. Losberne to the driver, climbing back into the carriage.

Following this bitter disappointment, grief and sorrow, once again, engulfed Oliver. After another fortnight, when spring had begun, the Maylies made preparations for leaving the house at Chertsey, for some months.

It was a lovely spot and Oliver loved his new life. Gradually, he forgot about his unhappy life at the workhouse. Spring

flew swiftly by and summer arrived; and suddenly, the happy days came to an end.

Rose fell very ill, unexpectedly.

Mrs. Maylie was alarmed on noticing a sudden change in the look of Rose one evening. By morning, Rose was in the first stage of a high and dangerous fever.

"Oliver, this letter must be sent to Dr. Losberne," said Mrs. Maylie. "Here is another letter, but I don't know whether to send it now, or wait until I see how Rose goes on."

"Is it for Chertsey, too, ma'am?" inquired Oliver, holding the letter in his trembling hands.

"No," replied the old lady, giving it to him mechanically. Oliver glanced at it and saw that it was directed to Harry Maylie, Esquire, at some great lord's house in the country.

"Shall this letter go, ma'am?" asked Oliver, looking up, impatiently.

"I think not," replied Mrs. Maylie, taking it back. "I will wait until tomorrow. But, my dear, you better hurry with the other letter."

Oliver ran as fast as he could towards the inn in town, four miles away, to give the letter to the postman to forward it further to Dr. Losberne. Swiftly, Oliver ran across the fields and down the little lanes. He did not stop even once, until he reached the little market place of the town.

Here, Oliver paused and looked about for the inn. He noticed a yellow town hall and in one corner there was a large house, bearing the sign of 'The George.'

Oliver ran towards the inn and spoke to a post-boy, who was dozing under the gateway. The boy, after hearing what he wanted, referred him to the innkeeper, who, after hearing everything, referred him to the landlord.

After ten minutes, Oliver finally saw the letter sent by 'speedy delivery'.

Oliver was coming out of the gateway when he accidentally stumbled against a tall man, who was coming out of the inn. The tall man was wrapped in a cloak.

"Hah!" cried the man, fixing his eyes on Oliver and suddenly recoiling. "What the devil's this?"

"I am sorry," stammered Oliver, confused by the strange man's wild look. "I hope I have not hurt you!"

"Rot you!" murmured the man between his clenched teeth. "What are you doing here?"

The man shook his fist as he uttered these words incoherently. Then, he advanced towards Oliver as if to hit him, but fell violently on the ground. And as he lay there, the man twitched and twisted, as if in a fit.

Oliver gazed in horror at the struggles of the man and then darted into the house for help.

When the man was safely carried into the hotel, Oliver turned his face homewards and ran as fast as he could to make up for lost time.

In the meantime, Rose's condition had grown, rapidly, worse. A medical practitioner, who resided in the country, constantly attended her. After first seeing the patient, he had taken Mrs. Maylie aside and told her that Rose's illness was serious.

"In fact," he said, "it would be a miracle if she recovered."

That night, Oliver could not sleep at all. Every small sound coming from Rose's room made him sit up and try to listen carefully and pray fervently for the kind and gentle girl.

Morning came and the little cottage was lonely and still. People spoke in whispers, anxious faces appeared at the gate, women and children went away in tears. All through the day, and for hours after it had grown dark, Oliver paced softly up and down the garden, raising his eyes every instant towards the sick chamber.

Late that night, Dr. Losberne arrived.

"It is serious," said the good doctor; "there is very little hope."

The sick girl was no better the next day.

Oliver crept away to the old churchyard and, sitting down on one of the green mounds, wept and prayed for her in silence.

When he reached home, Mrs. Maylie was sitting in the little parlor. Oliver's heart sank when he saw her sitting thus, for all these days she had never left the bedside of her niece and he trembled to think what change could have driven her away from Rose!

Both of them sat down in silence, afraid to speak, for hours. Their meals were brought and removed, untouched.

Suddenly, their quick ears caught the sound of an approaching footstep. Mrs.

Maylie and Oliver stood up, as Dr. Losberne entered the room.

"How is Rose?" cried the old lady. "Oh, tell me at once!"

"Be calm, my dear ma'am, please!" said the doctor, supporting her.

"Let me go!" cried Mrs. Maylie, with a desolate look on her face and struggling to free herself from the doctor's hold. "My dear child! She is dying!"

"No!" cried the doctor, passionately. "As he is good and merciful, she will live to bless us all, for years to come. Rose is out of danger."

It was almost too much happiness to bear! Oliver felt stunned and dazed by the unexpected news. He could neither weep, nor speak, nor rest. He just ran outside to gather the most beautiful flowers for Rose.

The night was fast closing in when Oliver returned homeward, laden with flowers, which he had gathered for Rose. Suddenly, he saw a post carriage coming along the road at great speed. As the horses were galloping on a narrow road, Oliver stood leaning against a gate until the carriage passed him.

The vehicle came to a halt before Mrs. Maylie's house, and Mr. Giles and a handsome young man stepped out of it. The young man was Mr. Harry Maylie, the son of Mrs. Maylie.

Harry Maylie rushed inside the house, where Mrs. Maylie was anxiously waiting to receive him.

"Mother!" whispered he; "Why did you not write to me before? What if her illness had been...had been fatal? You know that I wanted to..."

"My dear son," returned Mrs. Maylie, laying her hand upon Harry's shoulder, "You know Rose has a painful past, although through no fault of hers. If you marry her, malicious people will not allow you to forget that past. So, no matter how much you love Rose, you might repent your marriage one day. Then you will be hurting Rose too. Harry, I love Rose as much as I love you and I do not want any of you to be unhappy."

"Mother," said Harry, impatiently, "I could never, ever act in such a cowardly manner towards Rose. I love her! No mother, my mind is made up. I must speak to Rose about my feelings as soon as she has recovered enough to see me!"

The following evening, when the first shades of twilight were beginning to settle upon the earth, Oliver sat at a window, looking at his books. He had been poring over them for some time and gradually his eyes became heavy with sleep.

As he was dozing, suddenly, Oliver felt as if the scene had changed: the air became thick and confined and he thought that he was in Fagin's house again. Fagin was sitting in his accustomed corner, pointing at

Oliver and whispering to another man, who sat beside him.

Oliver thought he heard Fagin say, "Hush, my dear! It is definitely Oliver. Come away."

"Oliver!" the other man seemed to answer, "But what is he doing here?"

The man seemed to say this with such dreadful hatred, that Oliver awoke with fear.

Good Heavens! What was that? There, with his eyes peering into the room and looking at Oliver, stood Fagin! And beside him, white with either rage or fear, was the angry face of the man Oliver had met in the inn yard, when he had gone to send the letter to the doctor.

In another second, the men were gone. But they had recognized Oliver, and Oliver had recognized them. He stood transfixed for a moment; then, leaping from the window into the garden, he called loudly for help.

"It's Fagin! Help!"

Harry Maylie and Giles came running, when they heard Oliver's cries.

Mr. Giles failed to understand what Oliver was trying to say, but Harry Maylie, who had heard Oliver's history from his mother, understood it at once.

"What direction did they take?" he asked, picking up a heavy stick that stood in a corner.

"That way," replied Oliver, pointing the course the men had taken.

"Then they are in the ditch!" said Harry. "Follow me! And keep as close to me as you can."

Saying thus, Harry sprang over the hedge and darted off with a rapid speed, followed by Giles, Dr. Losberne, who had just returned from his walk, and Oliver.

However, the search went in vain. There were no traces of recent footsteps to be seen.

"It must have been a dream, Oliver," said Harry Maylie.

"Oh no, indeed, sir," replied Oliver, shuddering at the mere recollection of Fagin's face, "I saw him clearly. I saw them both, as plainly as I see you now."

"Who was the other?" inquired Harry and Dr. Losberne, together.

"The very same man I told you of, who came so suddenly upon me at the inn," said Oliver.

However, as there was nothing more that could be done, the three returned home.

That evening, when Oliver went to bed, he feared that since Fagin had found him, he would surely attempt to take him away. He was frightened, but at the same time he knew that the Maylies would never let Fagin take him back.

The next day, Harry went to have a talk with Rose, who had by now fully recovered. Harry and Rose were childhood friends and both shared great love and affection for each other. But when Harry told her of his wish to marry her, Rose refused.

"May I know the reason for your decision?" asked Harry.

"Harry, you know that there is a stain on my name and I do not want your ambitions to be harmed because of that," said Rose, as tears welled up in her eyes. "Your future is so bright. You should not spoil it! No, Harry, you must go!"

"I respect your wish, but I ask only one promise," said Harry. "Once, and only once more, say within a year, let me speak to you again on this subject, for the last time."

"Then let it be so," answered Rose, softly.

Rose extended her hand towards Harry. But the young man took her into his arms, tenderly kissed her beautiful forehead and hurried from the room.

Harry Maylie left for London the very next morning.

Chapter 15

Monks Meets Mr. and Mrs. Bumble

Meanwhile, Mr. Bumble had married Mrs. Corney and had become the master of the workhouse. However, in spite of his desires being fulfilled, Mr. Bumble was an unhappy man. His wife often quarreled with him, and once or twice, had even thrashed him with a broom!

One morning, two months after his marriage, Mr. Bumble walked out of his house after a fierce argument with his wife.

He boxed the ears of the boy who opened the gate for him and walked distractedly into the street. After wandering for a while, he entered a public house.

"I have seen you before, I think?" said a stranger on seeing Mr. Bumble. "You were the beadle of the workhouse once, were you not?"

"I was," said Mr. Bumble, in surprise. "But now I am the master of the workhouse, young man!"

The stranger smiled and nodded his head again.

"Now listen to me, carefully," said the stranger, in a low voice. "Today I had come here to find you and, by chance, you walked into the very room I was sitting in. I want some information from you. But I don't ask you to give it for free; tell me how much you want and I will pay it."

As he spoke, the man pushed a couple of sovereigns across the table towards Mr. Bumble, who gathered them up with much satisfaction.

The stranger went on further. "Carry your memory back to, let me see, twelve years ago, winter time."

"Very good. I've done it," said Mr. Bumble.

"The scene is the workhouse."

"Good!"

"And the time is night."

"Yes."

"A boy was born there, a meek-looking, pale-faced boy, who was apprenticed to a coffin-maker and who afterwards ran away to London."

"You mean Oliver Twist!" said Mr. Bumble.

"Yes! But it's not about him I want to hear," said the stranger. "It is about the woman who nursed his mother. Where is she?"

"She died last winter," answered Mr. Bumble.

The man appeared doubtful for a time as to whether he ought to be relieved or disappointed by the news. Then he rose, as if to leave.

At this point, Mr. Bumble informed the stranger, with an air of mystery that he knew a woman who was there with Old Sally when she died and maybe she could be of some help.

"Where can I find her?" cried the stranger.

"Only through me," answered Mr. Bumble.

"When?" cried the stranger, hurriedly.

"Tomorrow," replied Mr. Bumble.

The stranger took out a piece of paper and wrote down an address of a house by the riverside.

"Bring her to this place, nine o'clock in the evening."

Mr. Bumble glanced at the piece of paper and he found that no name was written on it.

"What name am I to ask for?" he asked.

"Monks!" answered the man and walked hastily away.

The next evening was dull, close and overcast. Mr. and Mrs. Bumble, turning out of the main street of the town, walked towards a scattered little colony of ruined houses. It was before one of those crumbling buildings that the couple paused.

"Hello there!" a man called out to them, from a door in the second storey of the building. "Stay right there. I'll be with you directly."

With these words the head disappeared and the door was closed.

"Is that the man?" asked Mr. Bumble's wife.

Mr. Bumble nodded in the affirmative.

The man, Monks, appeared in a moment and took them inside the building.

"This is the woman, is it?" demanded Monks, looking at the matron.

"Yes! That is the woman," replied Mr. Bumble.

Monks led them up some stairs to a shabby room and closed the window-shutter. In the dim light of the lantern, an old table and three chairs were visible in the room.

"Now," said Monks, when they all had seated themselves, "the sooner we come to our business, the better for everyone. The woman knows about the business, does she?"

Though the question was addressed to Mr. Bumble, it was his wife who replied, "Yes I do know."

"Well, then the first question is what did she tell you?" said Monks.

"That is the second. The first question is how much you are going to pay me in return for what I tell you?" observed Mrs. Bumble.

"How can I tell you without knowing what you are going to tell me? It may be worth nothing, or it may be worth twenty pounds," replied Monks.

"Give me twenty five gold sovereigns," said the woman, "and I'll tell you all I know. But not before that."

"Twenty five gold sovereigns!" exclaimed Monks, drawing back.

"It's not a large sum," replied Mrs. Bumble.

Mr. Bumble was quite frightened by his wife's boldness. However, Monks thrust his

Oliver Twist

hand into a side-pocket and, producing a canvas bag, took out twenty-five sovereigns, and pushed them over to the woman.

"Now," he said, raising his face from the table and bending forward, "let's hear your story."

The faces of the three nearly touched, as the two men leaned over the small table, in their eagerness to hear.

"When Old Sally died," the matron began, "she was alone with me."

"Was there no one else?" asked Monks.

"Not a soul," replied the woman; "I stood alone beside her when she died."

"Good," said Monks. "Go on."

"She spoke of a young woman who had given birth to a baby a few years before," resumed the matron, "on the same bed in which she lay dying. But Old Sally had robbed the mother of the child."

"While the woman was alive?" asked Monks.

121

"No, when she had died," replied the woman. "Old Sally stole what the dead mother had asked her to keep, for the infant's sake."

"Did she sell it?" cried Monks, with desperate eagerness. "Where? When? To whom?"

"Old Sally couldn't tell me anything more," said the matron. "She just fell back and died."

"And she didn't say anything else?" cried Monks. "It's a lie! I will kill you both!"

"It's the truth! She didn't utter another word," said the matron, "but I found a scrap of dirty paper in her hand. It was a duplicate of a money lender's script."

"Where is it now?" asked Monks, quickly.

"Here," replied the woman. And then, as if relieved of it, she hastily threw upon the table a small bag.

Monks immediately pounced upon the bag and tore it open with trembling hands.

The bag contained a small gold locket, in which were two locks of hair and a plain gold wedding ring.

"It has the word 'Agnes' engraved on the inside," said the matron. "There is a blank left for the surname and then follows the date which is within a year before the child was born. I found that out."

"Is this all?" said Monks, after a close and eager scrutiny of the contents of the little packet.

"All! Is that what you expected to get from me?" demanded the matron.

"It is," replied Monks.

"What do you propose to do with it? Can it be used against me?"

"Never," rejoined Monks, "nor against me either. I have nothing more to say to you and both of you can leave now. Light your lantern! And get away from here as fast as you can."

Chapter 16

A Wicked Plot is Discovered

The next evening, Monks went to meet Fagin. Nancy was also present at Fagin's place, for Sikes, who was a running fever, had sent her to get some money from him.

"Any good news?" inquired Fagin, as Monks walked through the door.

"Not bad, anyway," replied Monks. "I have been prompt enough this time. I want to have a talk with you, alone."

Oliver Twist

Although she could see that Monks was pointing to her, Nancy made no offer to leave the room and drew closer to the table. So, Fagin took Monks out of the room and led him to the second storey.

However, Nancy quietly followed them upstairs and listened at the door. She heard their entire conversation and hurried back downstairs. Soon afterwards, the two men descended the stairs, still absorbed in their conversation.

Monks went out at once into the street and Fagin crawled upstairs again to give Nancy money. When he returned, Nancy was adjusting her shawl and bonnet and she looked quite pale.

Fagin handed her the money, feeling miserable as he counted the coins into her hands. Then the two parted, after bidding each other a 'good-night.'

It was fortunate that Sikes did not observe Nancy's agitation, for he was only interested in the money she had brought him.

As that day closed in, the girl's excitement increased. And as night came on, and when Sikes was finally asleep, Nancy put on her shawl and bonnet and silently went out of the house.

Nancy gradually moved towards the wealthy quarter of the town. When she reached there, she found the streets comparatively deserted. In a while, Nancy reached her destination and gently knocked

on the door. She informed the doorman, who answered her knock, that she wanted to talk to Miss Maylie.

"What am I to say?" asked the man.

"That a young woman, earnestly, asks to speak to Miss Maylie, alone," said Nancy.

The doorman went inside with the message and in a little while, Rose appeared before Nancy.

"Sit down," said Rose, earnestly.

"Let me stand, lady," said Nancy, glancing around her nervously. "Is – is – that door shut?"

"Yes," said Rose. "Why?"

"Because," said the girl, "I am about to put my life and the lives of others, in your hands. I am the girl who dragged little Oliver back to old Fagin's house, the night he went out to return Mr. Brownlow's books."

"You!" cried Rose Maylie.

"Yes, lady!" replied the girl. "I am the wicked creature that lives among the thieves!"

"How dreadful!" exclaimed Rose.

"If you knew my story, you would pity me, young lady," said Nancy. "But I have come to tell you about some evil men and their dreadful plan. And they would surely murder me if they knew I had been here to tell you what I have overheard. Do you know a man named Monks?"

"No," said Rose.

"But he knows you," replied the girl; "and he knows that you live here. I myself heard him talk of this place, that is how I found you."

"I never heard the name," said Rose.

"Then he goes by some other name amongst us," answered the girl. "I began suspecting Monks soon after Oliver was put into your house for the robbery. I had overheard a previous conversation between him and Fagin. I deduced from the conversation that Monks had accidentally seen Oliver with two of our boys on the day we first lost him. He realized at once that the child he was looking for was Oliver, although I could not understand why. He immediately struck a bargain with Fagin, that if Fagin got Oliver back, he would receive a large sum of money. And if he managed to make Oliver a thief, he would get an even larger sum!"

"A thief!" cried Rose. "For what purpose?"

"Monks caught sight of my shadow on the wall as I tried to listen in the hope to find that out," said the girl, "and so I had to run away to escape recognition. Then, I saw him no more, until last night."

"And what happened last night?"

"I'll tell you, lady. Last night, Monks came again. Again Fagin and Monks went upstairs and I, stealthily, listened at the door. Monks said that the only proof of

Oliver's identity now lay at the bottom of the river. He also said that the old woman, who had received that proof, was no longer alive. Then he laughed out loud and told Fagin that he had got Oliver's money. But it would be more fun if Oliver was made a thief and sent to jail. And then, Fagin could easily manage to have Oliver hanged, after he had made a sufficient profit out of the boy!"

"What wickedness is all this!" exclaimed Rose.

"The truth, lady," replied the girl. "Then Monks swore that he would do anything to take Oliver's life himself, if there were no danger to himself. Monks then bragged to Fagin that nobody had ever laid such a trap, as he had planned, for his young brother, Oliver."

"His brother!" exclaimed Rose.

"Those were his words," said Nancy. "I must get back quickly now, or they will suspect me."

"But how do I help Oliver? Whom do I go and tell about it?"

"You must know some kind gentleman whom you can confide in and who will advise you what to do," answered Nancy.

"But where can I find you again when it is necessary?" asked Rose. "I do not want to know where these dreadful people live, but tell me a place and time where I can meet you."

"Will you promise me that you will keep my secret strictly and come alone, or with the only other person that knows it, and that I shall not be watched or followed?" asked Nancy.

"I promise you, solemnly," answered Rose.

"Every Sunday night, if I am still alive, I will walk across London Bridge from eleven, until the clock strikes twelve," said Nancy. Then, Nancy left.

Chapter 17

Oliver is Reunited with his Benefactor

fter Nancy had left, Rose sank into a chair, overpowered by the extraordinary interview. While she felt the most eager and burning desire to solve the mystery, which concealed Oliver's history, she could not betray Nancy's confidence and put her life at risk.

Rose was thinking, intently, over a course of action, when Oliver, who had been walking in the streets with Mr. Giles, entered the room breathless and in violent agitation.

"What makes you look so excited?" asked Rose.

"I have seen the gentleman," replied Oliver, scarcely able to speak clearly, "the gentleman who took care of me, whom we have so often talked about – Mr. Brownlow!"

"Where?" asked Rose.

"Getting out of a coach," replied Oliver, "and going into a house. I didn't speak to him – I couldn't speak to him, for he didn't

see me. I trembled so much that I was not able to go up to him. But Giles asked, for me, whether Mr. Brownlow lived there, and they said he did."

"Look here," said Oliver, opening a scrap of paper and showing Rose the address.

Rose read the address, which was Craven Street, in the Strand. She decided to go and meet the old gentleman.

"Quick!" she told Oliver. "Tell them to fetch a hackney-coach, and be ready to go with me. I will take you there directly, without further delay. I will tell my aunt that we are going out for an hour."

And in less than five minutes, the two were on their way to Craven Street. When they arrived there, Rose left Oliver in the coach and approached the house.

A servant answered the door. Rose told the servant that she had come to see Mr. Brownlow on important business.

Rose was shown into the study, where, after a while, an elderly gentleman of benevolent appearance, dressed in a bottle-green coat came to see her. Another old gentleman followed him. His hands were clasped on top of a thick stick.

"Dear me," said the gentleman in the bottle-green coat, with great politeness. "I beg your pardon, young lady, I kept you waiting. I beg you will excuse me. Please be seated."

"Mr. Brownlow, I believe, sir?" asked Rose.

"That is my name," said the old gentleman. "This is my friend, Mr. Grimwig."

"I shall surprise you very much, I have no doubt," said Rose; "but you once showed great kindness and goodness to a very dear young friend of mine and I am sure you will take an interest in hearing of him again."

"Indeed!" said Mr. Brownlow.

"His name is Oliver Twist," replied Rose.

Mr. Brownlow was speechless for a while. Then, collecting himself, he drew his chair nearer to Miss Maylie's, and said, "My dear young lady, if you have it in your power to produce any evidence that will change the unfavorable opinion towards that poor child, then I am eager to hear it."

"He is a child of a noble nature and a warm heart," said Rose.

Then, she related in a few words all that had befallen Oliver since he left Mr. Brownlow's house. She also told him how, during the past few months, Oliver had been upset because he was not able to meet his benefactor and tell him his sad tale.

"Thank God!" cried the old gentleman. "This is great news to me, great happiness! But you have not told me where he is now, Miss Maylie. Why did you not bring him along?"

"He is waiting in a coach at the door," replied Rose.

"At my door!" cried the old gentleman, as he jumped out of his chair and hurried out of the room, without uttering another word.

Soon, Mr. Brownlow returned with Oliver, whom Mr. Grimwig received very graciously. Mr. Brownlow then rang the bell for Mrs. Bedwin, the housekeeper.

As the old lady appeared, Oliver sprang into her arms.

"Oh dear!" cried Mrs. Bedwin, embracing him. "It is my innocent boy!"

Tears of joy streamed down the cheeks of the housekeeper.

Mr. Brownlow left Oliver and Mrs. Bedwin to talk at leisure with each other, while, he went into another room with Rose and his friend. Only then did Nancy narrate Oliver's entire story, which left Mr. Brownlow surprised and confused. It was then that they thought of a plan to rescue Oliver. They decided to take Dr. Losberne and Mrs. Maylie into confidence, but to say nothing to Oliver.

After a while, Rose and Oliver left, after promising to return the next day.

The next evening, Rose and Mr. Brownlow decided to meet Nancy on Sunday to get more information about Monks. Mr. Brownlow expressed his desire to seek the advice of Mr. Grimwig, while Dr. Losberne revealed his intention to seek the help of Harry. Mrs. Maylie postponed her trip abroad, until such time as the culprits were caught.

And thus, the course of action was finalized.

On the very Sunday night, when Rose Maylie went to meet Nancy, Noah Claypole and Charlotte left for London.

"Come on, can't you walk fast?" cried Noah. "Look there! Those are the lights of London."

"They're at least two miles off," said Charlotte, hopelessly.

"Never mind whether they're two miles off, or twenty," said Noah Claypole, "we will reach there very soon."

Charlotte, without any further remark, trudged onward by his side. They walked through narrow streets, keeping themselves away from the main road, for fear of being caught.

"Where are we resting for the night, Noah? I do not think my legs can carry me any further," Charlotte asked, after they had walked a few hundred yards.

"Now stop complaining," snapped Noah. "It is your fault that we had to take such a long route. It serves you right for being such a fool!"

"I know I am not as cunning as you are," replied Charlotte, "but I took the money for you Noah, dear."

"Did I keep it?" asked Noah Claypole.

"No, you trust me, and let me carry it," said the lady, drawing her arm through his.

Through the streets, Noah Claypole walked, dragging Charlotte after him, till they reached the inn called the 'Three Cripples.'

The innkeeper provided the tired travelers with some food. While the two were busy in their conversation, Fagin dropped by at the inn to inquire about one of his pupils.

The innkeeper, who had overheard Charlotte and Noah, pointed them out to Fagin. Fagin, too, sat down at a table next to them and tried to overhear them.

"So I mean to be a gentleman," said Noah, continuing the conversation, the beginning of which Fagin had arrived ,too, late to hear. "If you like, you shall be a lady."

"I should like that well enough, dear," replied Charlotte, "but cash boxes can't be emptied every day."

"There are a lot more things besides cash boxes to be emptied."

"What do you mean?" she asked.

"Pockets, houses, mail-coaches, banks!" said Noah Claypole.

"But you can't do all that alone, dear," cried Charlotte.

"I mean to get in with some gang," replied Noah, "And you can help me too, Charlotte."

After hearing the conversation, Fagin decided that the young man at the table was the right sort of person for him.

He directly went over to meet Noah and Charlotte. Striking a note of friendship with them, he invited Noah to join him in his profession, to which Noah readily agreed. The name that Fagin decided to bestow on Noah for his new profession was, Mr. Morris Bolter.

Chapter 18

Noah's Secret Mission

O n the same evening, Nancy sat listening to Sikes and Fagin discussing their plans. Finally, she got up to go out for a walk.

"Where are you going to?" asked Sikes.

"Just to have a breath of fresh air," Nancy replied.

"Open the window and hang your head out of it," snapped Fagin.

Nancy pleaded to them to let her go. But finally, when she saw that it was past midnight, she gave up the idea of going out.

That night, Fagin kept wondering about Nancy's strange behavior.

The next morning, he called in Noah. Now Fagin had planned a secret mission for Noah and so he had sent Charlotte away, with the other women of his gang.

"Bolter," began Fagin, "I want you to do a piece of work for me, my dear. This work

needs great care and caution. Your work is to spy on a woman."

"I can do that pretty well," said Noah. "Who is she?"

"One of us!" replied Fagin.

"Oh Lord!" cried Noah, curling up his nose.

"I believe that she has found some new friends and I must know who they are," said Fagin. "I'll point her out at the proper time. You just keep ready and leave the rest to me."

Fagin waited the entire week, and finally, on the seventh day he saw Nancy going out. He asked Noah to follow her.

The girl took a few restless turns to and fro from London Bridge. Then, at about midnight, a young lady, accompanied by a grey-haired gentleman, alighted from a hackney-coach at a distance from the bridge. Then they dismissed the vehicle and walked straight towards Nancy. They had scarcely set foot upon the pavement, when Nancy immediately rushed towards them.

"Not here," said Nancy, hurriedly. "Come away, out of the public road, down the steps over there!"

Noah managed to hide himself in the shadow of a wall and tried to listen to their conversation.

"You were not here last Sunday night," the gentleman told Nancy.

"I couldn't come," replied Nancy; "I was not allowed to go out."

"Did they suspect anything today?"

"No, they did not."

"Good," said the gentleman. "Now listen to me. This young lady has communicated to me and to some other friends who can be safely trusted, what you told her, nearly two weeks ago. All of us trust you and believe what you said. So, now we want you to bring Fagin to us."

"Fagin!" cried the girl, shrinking back.

"That man must be delivered up by you," said the gentleman.

"I will not do it!" replied the girl. "I know he has never treated me well, but I will never do that."

"But, why?"

"Because," answered the girl firmly, "like him, I too have led a bad life and he has never deceived me and I'll not deceive him."

"Then," said the gentleman, quickly, "put Monks into my hands and I will deal with him."

"What if he turns against the others?" asked Nancy.

"I promise you that if the truth is forced from Monks, the matter will rest there and the others shall go scot-free."

The girl thought for a while and then said, "I believe you."

"So what does Monks look like?" asked the young woman.

"He is a tall and strongly made man and he has a lurking walk. He is only twenty-eight years old, but his face is old and sunken. He often has terrible fits. As a result, his lips are purple and covered with marks. He is often spotted in the 'Three Cripples' inn. And one more thing! High upon his throat, so high that you can see a part of it below his neckerchief when he turns his face, there is …"

"A broad red mark, like a burn or scald?" cried the gentleman.

"Yes! How do you know that?" said the girl. "Do you know him!"

"I think I do," said the gentleman. "It must be him!"

"Young woman," the gentleman said, "you have been very helpful and I wish I could be of some help to you. Tell me, how can I help you?"

"You can't, sir. You can do nothing to help me," Nancy said, with a choked voice. Then, looking hastily round, she added, "I must go home now. We better part or someone might see us together. Go! Go! If I have done you any service, all I ask is that you leave me and let me go my way alone."

"Keep this money," said the young lady. "Take it for my sake, so that you may have some resource when you need it the most."

"No!" replied the girl. "I have not done this for money. Bless you! God bless you. Good-night!"

And thus they parted.

Noah stood still for some time and then rushed back to Fagin to tell him all that he had heard. The old man immediately sent for Sikes.

Sikes came carrying a bundle under one arm.

As he sat down, Fagin told him of Nancy's trip.

"You followed her?" cried out Sikes.

"Yes."

"To London Bridge?"

"Yes."

"Where she met two people?"

"A gentleman and a lady. They asked her to tell about her friends and especially about Monks, which she did. Then they asked her to describe Monks. She even told them about us."

"Hell's fire!" cried Sikes, furiously rushing out of the room.

"Bill, Bill!" cried Fagin, following him hastily. "Listen to me. You won't be too violent, Bill?"

Sikes made no reply but, pulling open the door, dashed into the silent streets. He walked straight on until he reached his own door.

Bill softly opened the door with a key and strode lightly up the stairs. He entered his own room and then double locked the door. Next, he placed a table against it and drew back the curtain of the bed.

Nancy was lying upon it.

"Get up!" said the man.

"Is it you, Bill!" said Nancy, with an expression of pleasure at his return.

"It is," was the reply. "Get up."

"Bill," said the girl, in a low voice of alarm, "why are you looking at me like that?"

The robber kept looking at Nancy for a few seconds, and then grabbed her by the head and throat. He dragged her into the middle of the room and covered her mouth with his heavy hand.

"Bill," gasped the girl, "I won't scream or cry, not once, hear me, speak to me, tell me what I have done!"

"You know what you have done!" hissed the robber, suppressing his breath. "You were followed tonight and every word you said was heard."

Then, grasping his pistol in one arm, he fired.

Nancy staggered and fell to the floor, covered in blood.

Bill stepped out of the room, locked it, descended the stairs and left his house.

He crossed the street and glanced up at the window to make sure that nothing was visible from the outside. Then he whistled at his dog, Bull's Eye, and walked away, rapidly.

Bill Sikes fled away from the scene and London. But fear haunted the wretched murderer everywhere he went. And so, at last, Bill Sikes decided to come back and remain in hiding, in London.

Chapter 19

Lost Relationships
are Found

M r. Brownlow got down from a
hackney-coach before his own
house. He knocked gently at the
door. When the door was opened,
a well-built man got out of the coach and
positioned himself on one side of the steps,
while another man got down from the coach
and stood upon the other side. Mr. Brownlow
gave a signal and the two men helped a third
man out of the coach and then they dragged

him into the house. This third man was none
other than Monks.

Although Monks had tried to rebel, once
Mr. Brownlow threatened to hand him over
to the police, he quietly sat down.

"Lock the door on the outside," said Mr.
Brownlow to his companions, "and come
inside when I ring."

The men obeyed and the two were left
alone together.

"This is nice treatment, sir," said Monks, "from my father's oldest friend."

"It is *because* I was your father's oldest friend," returned Mr. Brownlow, "that I treat you gently now, Edward Leeford."

"But what do you want from me?" said Monks.

"You have a brother," said Mr. Brownlow.

"I have no brother," replied Monks.

"I know about the unhappy marriage into which your poor father was forced by his family, when he was a mere boy. You were born out of that unhappy marriage."

"Well, my parents were separated," said Monks; "so what?"

"When they had been separated for some time," said Mr. Brownlow, "and your mother had utterly forgotten her young husband, your father made new friends. One of his friends had two daughters, one a beautiful girl of nineteen and the other a mere child two or three years old. This nineteen-year-old girl grew to love your father. Your father also fell in love with her."

"Your story is too long," observed Monks.

"But it is true!" cried Mr. Brownlow. "The death of your father occurred in the most mysterious circumstances. On his visit to Rome, your mother followed him and then he died mysteriously. Your mother said that your father did not leave any will; but I know he *did* leave one, for he had talked to me about it."

Now, as Mr. Brownlow narrated, Monks held his breath and listened with a face of intense eagerness.

"Before he went abroad," said Mr. Brownlow, "your father came to me."

"I never heard of that," interrupted Monks.

"He came to me and left with me a picture, a portrait, painted by him, of this girl, whom he was going to marry. Unfortunately, that was the last time I ever saw him. He never sent me any letters and after a few days, I was told that he was dead."

"A short while after his death, I tried to locate this young woman, for she was carrying his child. I had decided to take them home with me. But when I got to her father's home, I learned that the family had left London the week before."

Monks drew his breath.

"And then, a few years later, I happened to meet your brother, Oliver," said Mr. Brownlow. "A frail, ragged, neglected child was rescued by me. When he lay, recovering from sickness, in my house, I was shocked to see his strong resemblance to the picture of the woman your father left with me. But there is no need to tell you that the boy was taken away before I could find anything out about his history."

"Why not?" asked Monks, quickly.

"Because, you know it well!" answered Mr. Brownlow.

"I!"

"Yes, do not deny it. I know it was you who planned everything," cried Mr. Brownlow.

"You – you - can't prove anything against me," stammered Monks. "I defy you to do it!"

"We shall see," returned the old gentleman, with a penetrating glance. "I had lost the boy and I could not find him anywhere. Therefore, to find more about the young lad, I went to the West Indies. Once I reached there, I immediately went in search of you. But then I was told that you had left the place months before you were supposed to. So I returned and walked the streets day and night trying to find you. And look today, I have finally found you!"

"And now what do you plan to do with me? You do not have any proof that my father had another son. You can't do anything," said Monks, with a wicked smile.

"I did not know many things," replied Mr. Brownlow, rising, "but within the last fortnight, I have learnt it all. You have a brother and you know it. There was a will, which your mother destroyed, leaving the secret and the gain to you at her own death. It contained a reference to some child likely to be born. You knew about the child and you found him. There existed proof, proof long suppressed, of the child's birth and parentage. Those proofs were destroyed by you and now lie at the bottom of the river."

"Unworthy son, coward, liar, you, Edward Leeford, do you still deny the wrongs you have done to your brother?" cried Mr. Brownlow, furiously.

"No, no, no!" Monks cried out.

"Every word!" cried the gentleman, "every word that has passed between you and Fagin is known to me. A woman has been murdered and you are responsible for it."

"No, no," interposed Monks. "I - I knew nothing of the murder. I didn't know the cause. I thought it was a common quarrel."

"It was because your secrets were disclosed partially," replied Mr. Brownlow. "Now, tell me, will you disclose everything?"

"Yes, I will."

"And sign a statement of truth and facts and repeat it before witnesses?"

"I promise that too."

"Monks, you have to give your brother his rights. Though your father died before his birth, you will give him all that the will said."

"I will! I will!"

While Monks was pacing up and down the room, torn by his fears and his hatred, the door was quickly unlocked and Dr. Losberne entered the room in great fury.

"The man will be taken," he announced. "He will be taken tonight!"

"The murderer?" asked Mr. Brownlow.

"Yes," replied the other. "His dog was seen lurking somewhere. It seems his master is hiding away somewhere nearby. There are spies all around and I talked to the officer handling his case. He told me that Sikes would be arrested soon. The government has announced a reward of one hundred pounds for his arrest."

"I will give fifty more," said Mr. Brownlow. "Where is Mr. Maylie?"

"Harry? The moment he saw Monks with you, he hurried off to find Sikes."

"And what became of Fagin?" asked Mr. Brownlow.

"When I last heard, he was a free man, but by now I believe he has been locked up."

"Have you made up your mind?" Mr. Brownlow asked Monks.

"Yes," he mumbled.

"Remain here till I return. It is your only hope of safety."

Mr. Brownlow then left the room with Dr. Losberne, and locked the door from the outside.

Chapter 20

Sikes' Escape

In one of the corners of the city, three men sat in gloomy silence inside a house. One of these was Toby Crackit, another Mr. Chitling and the third, a robber, about fifty years of age, whose nose had been almost beaten in during some old fight. This man was an escaped criminal and he went by the name of Kags.

Toby Crackit turned to Chitling and said, "When did they take Fagin?"

"At about two o'clock in the afternoon. Charley and I escaped through the chimney and Bolter was captured."

"What happened to young Bates?" demanded Kags.

"He is hiding, he'll be here soon," replied Chitling. "There's nowhere else to go for now, for the people at 'Three Cripples' are all in custody."

Suddenly, the three men heard a pattering noise upon the stairs and Sikes's dog jumped inside the room from an open window. It was limping and its tongue lolled out with thirst and fatigue.

"It's Sikes' dog! I hope Sikes will not come here as well," cried Toby, as they gave the dog some water to drink.

After some time, when it had grown quite dark, they heard a sudden knocking at the door below. Crackit went down to the door. He returned with a man whose face was partially concealed by a handkerchief. The remaining part of the face was hidden under a hat. Slowly, he showed his face.

It was Sikes, having a blanched face, sunken eyes, hollow cheeks, three days' beard and a wasted, thin body. He rested his hand upon a chair that stood in the middle of the room and sat down. All three men in the room, except Sikes, remained silent and no one said a word to the newcomer.

There was an eerie silence throughout the room. Then, suddenly, there was another knock at the door and once again Crackit went to answer the knock. He returned with Charley Bates.

As soon as Charley's eyes fell on Sikes, he became horrified.

"You monster!" he cried, "Fiend! If they come after you, I will give you up. I am not afraid of you! Murderer! Help!"

Pouring out these cries and accompanying them with violent gestures, the boy actually threw himself, single-handed, upon the strong man and brought him heavily to the ground.

The three spectators seemed quite stupefied. They offered no interference and the boy and man rolled on the ground together.

Suddenly, there came a loud knock at the door accompanied with a number of angry voices from below. Strokes, thick and heavy, rattled upon the door and the lower window-shutters.

Amid all this confusion, out came a voice that offered a reward of fifty pounds to anyone who would catch the murderer alive. Tempted by the offer and anxious to capture the criminal, the crowd broke down the door of the house and went inside.

Meanwhile, Sikes made a last attempt to escape. He climbed onto the roof of the house, carrying a rope. However, as he climbed on the roof, he lost his balance and the rope caught around his neck. As he fell down, the noose around his neck got tighter and tighter. And finally, with a jerk, the foul murderer was hanged against the wall of the house, by his own doing.

Chapter 21

A Family Reunited

Two days after this incident, at three o'clock in the afternoon, Oliver was in a traveling-carriage rolling fast towards his native town. Mrs. Maylie, Rose, Mrs. Bedwin and the good doctor were his companions. Mr. Brownlow followed them in a post-carriage, accompanied by one other person.

They drove straight to the door of the chief hotel, and here stood Mr. Grimwig, all ready to receive them.

Soon, everybody gathered in the dining hall and ate their dinner. However, Mr. Brownlow did not join them at the meal, but sat alone in a separate room. The two other gentlemen hurried in and out with anxious faces, and, during the short intervals when they were present, conversed apart. Once, Mrs. Maylie was called away. She remained absent for nearly an hour and when she came back her eyes were swollen with weeping. All this made Oliver and Rose nervous and uncomfortable. But they sat wondering, in silence.

At last, around nine o'clock, Dr. Losberne and Mr. Grimwig entered the room, followed by Mr. Brownlow and a man. This man was Mr. Brownlow's brother.

Monks looked with hatred at all of them and sat down in a corner. Mr. Brownlow, who had some papers in his hand, walked to a table near where Rose and Oliver were seated.

"This child," began Mr. Brownlow, drawing Oliver to him, "is your half-brother, the son of your father, my dear friend Edwin Leeford. His mother was Agnes Fleming, who died while giving birth to him."

"Yes," said Monks, scowling at Oliver.

"And now Monks," said Mr. Brownlow, "why don't you tell the rest of the story."

"All right then, listen!" cried Monks. "Our father fell ill in Rome. My mother and he were separated then. My mother went to meet him in Rome. The next day he died. There were two letters and a will. One letter was for Oliver's mother, whom he intended to marry, and the other was for Mr. Brownlow. In the letter to this woman, he begged her forgiveness for not being able to marry her."

"Where is the will? What was there in it?" said Mr. Brownlow, as Oliver started crying.

But Monks kept silent.

"The will," said Mr. Brownlow, speaking for Monks, "left you and your mother each an allowance of eight hundred pounds. He divided his entire property into two equal portions, one for Agnes Fleming and the other for their child."

"My mother," spoke up Monks, "did what a woman should have done. She burnt this particular will. The letters never reached their destination. Oliver's mother had left her home, in secret, some weeks before. And she gave birth to Oliver in the parish workhouse."

There was a short silence here, and then Mr. Brownlow said, "Years after this happened I was visited by the mother of this man, Edward Leeford, also known as Monks. He had left her when he was only eighteen, robbed her of money, gambled and fled to London. She was suffering from an incurable disease and wished to find him before she died. Then after a long search, Monks was found and she took him back to France."

"There she died," said Monks, "after a long illness. Before she died she told me all the secrets. She felt strongly that Agnes might have given birth to a boy. So I came to London in search of the boy and took the help of Fagin and his group to ruin the boy completely."

"What about the locket and the ring?" said Mr. Brownlow, turning to Monks.

"I bought them from the man and woman I told you about. They had stolen them from a nurse who had in turn stolen them from Agnes," answered Monks, without raising his eyes.

Mr. Brownlow glanced at Mr. Grimwig, who immediately went out. He shortly returned, pushing in Mrs. Bumble and her husband.

"Oh Oliver! Is it you little Oliver? Oh! I have been looking for you Oliver!" cried Mr. Bumble.

"Do you know that person?" asked Mr. Brownlow, pointing towards Monks.

"No," replied Mrs. Bumble, flatly.

"Perhaps you don't know him either?" said Mr. Brownlow, addressing her husband.

"I never saw him in all my life," answered Mr. Bumble.

"So you mean to say that you never sold him a ring and a gold locket."

Again Mr. Brownlow nodded to Mr. Grimwig and again that gentleman limped away. He shortly returned with two women who had attended Old Sally as she lay dying. "We heard everything that Old Sally told you about. We also saw you take that paper out of Sally's hand. We followed you the next day and saw you enter a pawnbroker's shop," one of the ladies told Mrs. Bumble.

"Yes," added the second, "and it was a 'locket and a gold ring'. We found out that these two items were given to you. We saw everything! We saw it in your hand!"

"Would you like to see the pawnbroker himself?" asked Mr. Grimwig as he gestured towards the door.

"No," replied Mrs. Bumble; "I have nothing more to say. I did sell them and they're where you'll never get them."

"You may leave the room," said Mr. Brownlow.

And with this, Mr. Bumble and his wife left the room as fast as their feet could carry them.

Mr. Brownlow turned towards Rose and, holding her arm said, "My dear, now there are a few things you should know."

"Do you know this young lady, sir?" Mr. Brownlow asked, looking at Monks.

"Yes," replied Monks.

"But I have never seen you before," said Rose, faintly.

"I have seen you often," replied Monks.

"Agnes had a sister," put in Mr. Brownlow. "What happened to that child?"

"When the child's father died all of a sudden," replied Monks, "she was taken by some poor cottagers, who looked after her and brought her up as their own daughter."

"Go on," said Mr. Brownlow, "Go on!"

"Mr. Brownlow, you were not able to locate the place where Agnes' father and sister went, but my mother found them. She also found the small girl," said Monks.

"She took the child, did she?" asked Mr. Brownlow.

"No. The people who had taken up the child were poor. My mother gave them some money and took the child with her. And finally, the child was taken from my mother by a widow in Chester, who took pity on the small one."

"Do you know where she is now?"

"Oh, yes. She is in this very room, leaning on your arm," said Monks.

Mrs. Maylie was in a state of shock on hearing all this.

She rushed to Rose.

"Oh my dear niece!" she cried, holding Rose in her arms. "Oh dear, how happy I am for you! My sweet companion, my own dear girl!"

Rose, who was too shaken to say anything, began to cry, clinging to Mrs. Maylie.

"My heart will burst," she sobbed. "I cannot bear all this."

"Calm yourself, my love, look at this poor child who is waiting to hold you in his arms. Look at him."

"She is not my aunt! She is my sister!" cried Oliver, throwing his arms about Rose's neck. "I'll never call her aunt! She is my sister, my own dear sister. Rose! Dear, darling Rose!"

In that one bittersweet moment, broken hearts were mended. Everyone shed tears of joy as lost ones found their family. And at that very moment, Harry Maylie entered the room. He came towards Rose and reminded her about her promise to consider his proposal one last time.

However, Rose was hesitant still and said that she was even more unworthy than before to marry him.

"No," declared Harry. "If my world cannot be yours, then I will make yours mine! I have nothing to do with those relatives who isolate themselves from me because of you. I know that I only want you. I will marry you, dear Rose, and settle down in the countryside."

Chapter 22

One Last Glance

he courtroom was crowded with people. It was as if the entire city had gathered there. And all looks were fixed upon only one man - Fagin.

The judge had given his verdict. Fagin was sentenced to be hanged.

Oliver felt sad when he heard about Fagin's sentence. Although Fagin had almost ruined him, Oliver could not forget that it was Fagin who gave him shelter and food to eat, when he had none. Oliver's kind heart sent a silent prayer for the wretched man.

Three months passed by.

Rose Fleming and Harry Maylie got married. They bought a beautiful house in the countryside and lived happily. Mrs. Maylie also lived with them in the country.

Oliver got his share in his father's property, according to the will, and Monks inherited the other half. However, Monks

went away to some distant land, fell into his old ways again and squandered away all his money. In the end, he landed himself in jail.

Among the other gang members of Fagin's group, only Charley Bates escaped a life of crime. He worked hard, and in time, he became an honest and respectable citizen.

Noah Claypole was granted pardon as he had testified against Fagin in the courtroom. He was granted pardon for all his crimes. Ultimately, he became a police informer and earned his living in this manner.

Mr. and Mrs. Bumble lost their position at the workhouse, and were reduced to a state of misery. They had to live as paupers in the same workhouse where they had once ruled over others.

Mr. Brownlow adopted Oliver as his son and upon Oliver's wish, they went away to stay in his father's house along with Mrs.

Bedwin. Mr. Brownlow educated Oliver in the best possible manner. With each passing day, Mr Brownlow became more attached to Oliver and grew to love him like a son.

The orphan, who once lived a miserable life in the workhouse, had finally left his old life behind. He had also, at long last, found affection, happiness and a loving family.

A stone tablet, bearing the name 'Agnes', stood near the altar of the old village

church. If the spirits of the Dead ever come back to earth, drawn by the love of their cherished ones, then perhaps the spirit of Agnes sometimes hovered round that solemn corner, looking down on her dear Oliver with love and pride.

THE END